The Town of Mohaba

The Town of Mohaba

Part 1 Death

NAZARIN MARZBAN

H&H

Ormond Beach
Florida USA

Credits

Cover work : Fabrizio Catalfamo

Editing : Hoffmann & Hoffmann

Publisher: Hoffmann & Hoffmann, LLC

9000 Saint Georges Road, 206 b

Ormond beach, Florida, US

ISBN-13: 978-1-947488-10-6
ISBN-10: 1-947488-10-4

Dedication

"When I want to read a novel, I write one."

Benjamin Disraeli

I dedicate this book to my Mother who believed that I could write when I asked her for the first time at age 5. Ever since then, the door to build my dream became unlocked. I will never forget that day.

1

THE TOWN OF MOHABA

W e kept hoping the sun would shine over the trees again. Instead, the dark miserable clouds that spread from the mountains out over the town remained. Mohaba's residents had gotten used to the ugly weather, unending rains, and dark gray clouds. How would their town be bright when demons possessed every corner of it? It had not been a pleasant place to live for its people, their parents, grandparents and even their great-grandparents.

Some of the people ran away in the hopes of finding a neighboring town. The ones remaining had no access to any news. They did not know if their friends, neighbors, or family members who managed to get away were alive or dead. I know what happened to them. None of them survived. They were the lucky ones. The unlucky ones were the ones who were left behind. Like them, I worried for my survival after many failed attempts to save Mohaba. I discovered that I could not protect them if I could not protect myself. No choice remained considering what would be at stake. Without me on the earth, there would be no life after death.

Strange things began to happen in Mohaba after the takeover of evil souls, known as the Devols. Residents opened their doors to be confronted by monsters. Rumors spread about horrible things happening inside and outside everyone's homes. Most people cowered inside their houses. They sentenced themselves and their families to live in the shadows. They avoided becoming prey.

The town that had once been so beautiful that life could be seen in everything that moved lay in the shadow of evil. It is astonishing to me how its humans survived centuries of torture. I guess they never felt the need to migrate elsewhere. Most of them had not known any better. They did not know about the outside world. They got used to Mohaba's depressing weather, unaware of the town's magical past.

There were no more luminous sunny days making the apple trees glow in Mohaba. All the apples were gone, eaten by worms, and the remains had turned into dried up seeds. Only sounds of grief and sadness permeated the town. Soon after the Devol's insurrection, Mohaba's shiny blue sea turned gray, the wild waves dulled as the sun vanished. The profound salt smell in the air annoyed the senses and muted emotions. The sands blinded while inside the ocean, heaven still existed. The external darkness hid the beauty hiding under the surface while the depressing clouds covered the entire town from the seashore to its far borders.

Days quickly turned into decades. I had not imagined these evil beings to be anything more dangerous than a tornado moving violently through the air. I believed to be the strongest force in the spirit world. I did not dare to battle with them alone. They discovered a way to take over any living being other than their own kind.

Soon, I found myself taking care of the souls of the deceased instead of saving them. Mohaba was viewed by the Devols, as a region to guard against any godlike creatures. No heaven existed if they protected the only district that held sacred treasures threatening their existence. Humans felt the Devols as a cold wind passing through. To afterlife and immortal souls, they appeared visible. Most of them looked like black ghosts and murky clouds wafting through the air. At night, their red eyes shone with yellow fires. It revealed if they possessed a creature. Over the centuries, some of their possessed animals adapted into a Devol.

Black hyenas had become the Devol's favorite animals. Anyone who walked outside risked death in the jaws of the hyenas. Some men and women discovered secret places to hide. These brave souls risked their lives by delivering food to the homes of barricaded families. They wore dark gowns to blend into the darkness that permeated the town. They passed groceries through tiny openings at the base of each home's front door, each item handed through one by one.

The forest creatures of Mohaba were the least lucky of all.

Unlike the residents, they had nowhere to hide. The Devols easily smelled them in their lairs. They stole their souls to viciously exploit them for their own devilish pleasures. Many of the wild animals were killed while their bodies were possessed by the malicious beasts. Many of the lions, chimpanzees, black bears, tigers, and wild dogs were stirred to battle against each other. To the Devols, it was all a sport. After the entertainment, I had to quietly carry the tortured souls of the bodies abandoned on the muddy floor of the forest. I transformed them into sea creatures in the hope they would find peace under the waters. No Devols dared to venture there.

I had been away for a few days when the Devols descended on Mohaba. They took possession like jackals attacking a young gazelle separated from its herd. I had not noticed the warning signs. If I had, I would have returned to Mohaba. Perhaps, I could have prevented the attacks. Sadly, at that time, loss of Mohabat consumed me deeply to care about our town. I assumed Mohaba would be safe, guarded by the angel tree souls. They would call out for me in the case of any danger. They must have been distracted by the mourning of Mohabat whom I had never let out of my sight before. Mohabat now belonged to the warriors of the spirit world. She was no longer mine.

One day, everything changed. I remember the day it happened. I had somewhat of a hope it would turn out sunny like the old days. Instead, thunder rolled swiftly over Mohaba. I moved to a higher tree, concerned lightning would strike a helpless citizen. Rather, it hit a mansion at the far end of the town. This now visible place, Jewl, seemed blocked from the view of passersby. To my surprise, it had been hidden from my sight.

I remembered Jewl being built, decades ago, by a man named Kerman. He was a man with a vision. At the time, most people in Mohaba lived in tents. They lived this way until they could cut enough wood to build a crude house for their family. They watched enviously as Kerman built this grand mansion. Sadly, by the time it was completed, the poor man had become old to enjoy it. I remember him struggling up to his stairs to the master bedroom from where he peered suspiciously out its small windows. Despite its beauty, Jewl had a desolate air about it.

Soon after his passing, Kerman's grandchildren disappeared behind Jewl's gates. They never shared their wealth nor treasures with anyone. Jewl did not seem to be the only place in Mohaba to possess many treasures valuable to the ones in the afterlife. Many precious beings valued to the spiritual world lived in our town. This might be why Mohaba attracted a lot of beasts, demons, angels, ghosts and other living and nonliving creatures.

Unknown treasures outside of Mohaba also existed in the other areas of the planet and galaxy waiting to be discovered. However, at the time, the town of Mohaba seemed to attract most of the spiritual creatures. I spent a lot of time there too. I had to ensure the spirit Mohabat stayed safe in the woods.

It did not matter what life demanded of me elsewhere. With one blink of an eye, I would be back in Mohaba.

I feared not only the Devols, but also the more powerful Baduevols. They belonged to the same hyena family-line but were much bigger. With the black hyenas, they ruled the night. They viciously exerted their powers over Mohaba for years. They were firmly loyal to the Devols. After the storm, countless numbers of them had gathered around Jewl.

The Baduevols guarded and surrounded the mansion while the Devols blanketed it with dark clouds. The unexpected lightning burnt the bushes around Jewl. The flames spread to nearby forests, attracting everyone's attention. The people soon began to believe the thunder vanished with only the dark clouds remaining in the sky. They had no clue that the Devols attempted to hide the grandiose Jewl. The Devols made it appear to be the ordinary aftermath of a thunder-storm.

However, a glimmer of hope remained as the Devols failed to fool us completely. The mansion remained visible to us despite the Devol's every attempt to hide it. We had never known them to waste time on anything this vigorously. This made us wonder about their intent. It could only mean that they were hiding something that could damage their exis-tence. I became concerned with what was hidden inside the castle. Kerman's family disappeared in there long ago. There were no signs of life but plenty of valuable treasures — plenty of gold, jewelry, tapestries, and unique items.

Mohaba's spirit world heard the rumors about the Devols

and Jewl. Sadly, they did not dare to investigate it more deeply. The spiritual warriors, known as the Angelious, treated Mohaba as their only home. They practiced their battling skills every day in its forested mountains. Unlike the Devols, the Angelious were warrior souls belonging to the good. They lived in secrecy for centuries. They gradually metamorphosed into a legion of powerful spirits. Mohabat had become their leader, respected for her strength and kindness. They called her, "Miss Mohabat". Her name is all that she could remember. Other clues to her past included the clothes she wore while she joined the other Angelious in the forest. Her cohorts knew nothing of Mohabat's past because they, too, had been transformed into Angelious upon the moment of death.

Buddha, my friend since his passing, lived secretly away in Mohaba's forests. Thousands of years ago, he earned his immortal soul. This made it possible for us to be friends. He could live as flesh and blood. I had no control over the gods' greater plans for him. I heard their wishes for Buddha to continue applying his rules to both the living and non-living. Buddha and I made a pact to never reveal his identity unless it was mutually agreed upon.

My friendship with Buddha evolved fast. We had similar interests. Subjects such as human birth, death and reincarnation are amongst Buddha's greatest passions. Therefore, he is a good friend. No one sees us but we do make a difference. Buddha counsels me often, "No matter how hard the past Mahboo, one can always begin again. You must believe it is possible. You are not alone in this world. Mohabat may be gone to you but she is here, isn't she? Be grateful for that. Continue staying strong for the people of Mohaba. They need you."

Buddha has many gifts and being an expert of karate is one of his many great talents. Although while human, he hid his ability from others, he now applies it as an immortal Buddha. He is a strong spirit, which makes it easy for him to connect to any creature, including the Angelious. Over the centuries, Master has worked with many strong teams of monks. And every day, he works to strengthen his mental and physical skills. He meditates often to stay calm and focused and to get closer to himself. It helps him maintain a peaceful mind.

Over the years, Buddha shared his wisdom with many in need of guidance. He views happiness as not something bounded by disasters created by enemies but as something within the power of the mind. He taught me how to balance my everyday struggles. He helped me cope with ongoing dilemmas created by the Devols. He cautioned me, "Mahboo, remember even the deepest pool can rot if no action is taken. The only real failure in life is not to be true to one's self."

The thunderstorm occurred while Master was in deep meditation. I interrupted his meditation, unable to wait to deliver the news. Buddha did not appear mad at me for interrupting his silence. He rose from his seated position, pushing himself up from the hard ground with his left arm. As he stood in front of me, relief from centuries of disappointment appeared on his face. He silently gazed at me. I noticed his eyes opened wide to a new window of hope.

With no doubt, Buddha was the strongest being in the spiritual world. Over the many years of failure to defeat our enemy, even he had almost given up hope. I felt a strong rush of air. After a short silence, Master spoke. He warned me, "The time has come, my friend, for us to come out of our shells for Mohaba's sake."

"I could not agree more."

"Yes, now that we have discovered the Devol's weak spot, we have to do whatever it takes."

"I believe we can now."

"We would need to act fast, of course."

"No doubt. Do you believe the gods had a part in creating the lightning? Maybe it was not an accident. But, why did it take them so long?"

"Listen, Mahboo. We cannot focus on the past. We cannot afford to spend hours hoping to figure out why things happened the way they did."

"True."

Buddha walked back towards the wall of his cave. He took a double-edged sword from a collection on his wall. I acted fast. I reached for a carved wooden pen and, as Buddha spoke, recorded his plan, step-by-step, for attacking Jewl.

But, to my surprise, Buddha did not focus much on Jewl. Instead, with the sword gripped tightly in both hands, Master turned around and scratched out, on the ground, an image of a woman seated in a yoga pose.

"This is what we need to do first." And with that, Master began to talk about Mohabat, the one subject that I avoided. "Mahboo, the time has come."

"Yes, indeed."

"No, I mean the time has come."

"I know Master, I know it has."

"No Mahboo. When I said, the time has come, I meant, the time has come for you to reunite with …"

"But …" I suddenly felt a breeze, strong enough that it silenced me but not the swirling thoughts in my head. My whole body remained in shock. For a moment, I could not move or talk.

I only recall watching Buddha talk. I did not hear a thing he said. My mind was coming to terms with the idea of having to face a warrior who owned my heart. When my voice returned to me, I spoke haltingly, "You mean Mohabattehehhh."

Master moved close and placed his hand on my right shoulder. "Mahboo, did you hear what I said?"

"I need to think about this."

"Yes, you do and quickly." Buddha looked concerned. It seemed, for a moment, to forget about our enemies and Jewl. He then took his hand away from my shoulder and a step back. He looked deeply into my eyes, "I have never seen you like this. Are you not happy this day has come my friend?"

"How can I not be?"

"Well then."

"It is just that it is all too difficult to bear, that is all. I mean, what if I lose her again."

"You cannot think like that."

"She is safer in the woods unknown, you know. She is undetected by other souls."

"Mahboo, you do not recall why you turned her into an Angelious?"

"To be honest, no."

"What do you mean?"

"Devols did not exist at the time. I knew she had enemies. But, a power within me, maybe the gods, decided her fate, not me."

"I see. It does not matter who decided her fate."

"True, right."

"What matters is that she is the strongest leader of Mohaba's forests and whether you like it or not, we need her for battle."

"But, I think we can do this without their help. Why can't we try without them first?"

"Mahboo, you have done a great job protecting Mohabat all these years."

"Exactly, that is exactly why I fear involving her in this."

"But, you knew they are warriors after all. They would one day participate in a war with us."

"That is true."

"We have no other choice. After all, it is the Angelious who are the best fighters in Mohaba."

"But Master, we both know you have created a great team of fighters yourself. Your team is better, stronger."

"Yes, but my students have tragic pasts and are human. Angelious have a better chance at survival than my students no matter how talented and strong I have made them."

"You are right." I turned and walked towards the figure Buddha had sketched with his sword. I thought about his war plan and our battle team.

"We both knew this day would come. I thought you would be happy."

"I am sorry, Master."

"It is all right."

"No, it is not. You are right. We longed for this day and now here it is. We cannot waste time. We have no other choice." The idea of having to face Mohabat now, after all, the years apart, terrified me. I pictured the possibility of winning the war. I envisioned while looking at the image of the seated warrior, how our victory would be an answer to all our prayers. We would all finally have our chance to a better future.

Buddha recognized my pain although it had been long before his time when Mohabat entered my world. He understood my agony. I witnessed her dripping blood until nothing remained of her except a fading ghost. If Master blamed me as I blamed myself, I undoubtedly would have abandoned Mohaba without looking back. Luckily, that was not the case. But Buddha decided that the time had come for me to meet with Mohabat. One thing remained certain, I could not disobey.

Buddha reported, "I have been watching the Angelious practicing karate from afar. However, I question their strength."

"I actually do too. They need to strengthen their skills a bit more with more practice."

"Well, not quite. It is not their skills per se. I have no doubts about their abilities. I have observed their practices. They are talented. I noticed something missing."

"What precisely?"

"Their weakness is in their hearts." Though they believed they were invisible souls, ghosts with no hearts, the warriors had hearts. Sadly, they never pondered their internal hearts.

"I see. Is there something we can do to help them?"

"We do not have much time. I am positive with intense practice, we can help them develop stronger hearts. This will make them less vulnerable to the Devols."

"I agree. I trust you have a plan."

"I think I do. We must act fast. We do not have a lot of time."

"I understand. I will assist you in every way I can Master even if it means I have to face Mohabat."

"Alright, I do not doubt the Angelious' warrior skills. Mohabat has done well training them. We need to focus on strengthening their hearts."

"I think so too. I think I am ready now to wage war with the Devols."

"Glad to hear."

"Well, that is when the time comes, which I hope is soon." That day seemed at last close now that the Devols were all in one spot.

The stories of the Devols holding souls captive spread throughout the spirit world. With Jewl's location revealed, Buddha and I aimed to disable the Devols' powers and regain Mohaba. We decided that the time had come to join forces with Mohabat's team. We needed more than Buddha's help to win the upcoming battle. With the help of Buddha's students and the Angelious, we were going to save Mohaba from captivity. We knew we could return it to the good souls.

Buddha knew the pain of my separation from Mohabat. Things were going to be quite different this time. This time, Mohabat was not human. I knew the best strategy would be for Buddha to become acquainted with her before practice began.

Shortly after making our decision, Buddha disguised himself as a monk to visit Mohabat in her forest home. His spiritual powers enabled him to find her exact location. He wore the same robe in which he had passed away many centuries ago. His robe, like those of many homeless holy men, had been patched together from rags cut from pure abandoned cloth. It had been previously worn by someone who had passed away. Buddha had dyed it in boiled saffron and turmeric to eliminate any bacteria. It turned it into orange hue color that marked a person wearing it as a monk.

Master startled Mohabat as she gazed at the dark clouds

over Mohaba. Buddha felt guilty for frightening her. He detected her fear and her suspicion that he might be a Devol. He fretted, "I apologize if I have scared you. I can assure you that I am not a Devol. There is an urgent matter I need to discuss with you but not here."

"Please back away."

"I reassure you if you allow me to explain. I am a real monk."

"No need."

"If you wish, you can analyze my cloth. You will be able to tell from the ingredients it is made from."

"You are trying to trap me. But do not mistake me for a fool."

"I work at the rescue center. Perhaps you remember me from there."

"Oh, now that you mentioned, yes, that is right, we have met before."

"Yes, although we have never spoken. Perhaps that is why you do not recall me. I am told my voice sounds different from what people expect by looking at me." Buddha started to gain confidence as he noticed the conversation was beginning to go well.

"I am sorry. I do remember you now."

"That is all right."

"How could I not? I mean, I have seen you at the rescue center many times. I have seen what a wonderful work you are doing there, it is honorable."

"That is kind of you to say."

"I am terribly sorry for not remembering you. I cannot trust anyone around me. I hope you can understand."

"I do. It is understandable."

"I know but I should be fearless. I do not understand why we cannot be stronger than them?"

"What we have is now. We can become stronger than them."

"I thought they had no brains, no ability to reason as we do."

"That is true. But sometimes, things can be out of our hands. It is how we cope with such problems that are important. I am certain this time, we finally have our chance."

"We do? How?" Surprised Mohabat asked. She identified the monk's holy power. Mohabat knew he was devoted to the people of Mohaba. She doubted his ability to fight the evil spirits.

"If there is a will, my dear, there is always a way. You have heard that saying?"

"Yes, I have."

"Good. We all want the Devols gone. We have the will to fight them and now we have our chance with Jewl as our clue."

"Do you think Jewl is the answer?"

"Yes, I do. Why else would they be protecting it so intensely?" Buddha paused for a moment. Mohabat looked back at the darkened clouds. She pondered how they could ever defeat the Devols. Buddha followed her eyes, wondering about the truth of his own words. Still, he was determined to show no fear. He regained his positive attitude. He had to convince Mohabat that this time, they would win.

After gazing at the black fogs, Mohabat decided to trust the man in the orange robe. She followed him to his place where Buddha then revealed his true self. Mohabat became cheerful to Buddha's surprise. She had known the human form of Buddha well. She used to observe him while he sat under his favorite tree teaching his believers.

Buddha acquainted Mohabat with his best karate techniques. Mohabat quickly picked up. After spending some time inside Buddha's cave, Buddha urged Mohabat. "You know we are risking our covers. We have to be careful whom we trust."

"I have no problem with risking it all, if that will help Mohaba."

"Well done, my lady."

Mohabat enjoyed hearing Buddha call her 'my lady'. It meant he valued her. She showed gratitude. "Thank you. It means a lot to see how much you believe in me."

"Of course, I believe in you more than you know. You are special. You will one day discover how special you are." Buddha stated with a strong tone of voice. "I have seen what a great leader you are. Your fighting skills are incredible."

"Thank you. You are too kind." She walked towards Buddha's wall.

"You can handle any of the swords you like."

"I wish we knew what is hiding behind those dark walls." Mohabat continued checking the swords hanging on Buddha's wall. She smiled, "I am not going to pick one. You are a wise man. You are testing me."

"No, I mean it. Please choose one. It is my gift to you. It is my way of showing you my appreciation for helping us."

"I have to say; your swords are unique. I have never seen swords like these before."

"Thank you, my lady. I did spend a great deal of time making them."

"You made these?"

"Yes, I have. They are each made with my own hands."

"Your immortal hands, of course."

Buddha laughed, "Yes, with my bare immortal hands."

"I cannot believe this. How do you find the time in addition to working at the rescue center, meditating, practicing karate, training your monks and teaching your students?"

"I do not always. The meditation helps me focus. After my meditation, if I have time, I work on one of the swords. I need to focus so I can make the sword strong, flexible, hard and balanced."

"It is because of the Devols that you make them, is it not?"

"Yes, I have prepared them in the hopes that ..."

Mohabat rushed in to ask, "Will your students be using them?"

"Yes, indeed. They can kill the hyenas with these."

"Not on their own."

"With our help, they can."

"I hope so." Mohabat sighed. "I am grateful to have met

you. I will be honored to work with your team. You have convinced me that together, we can fight the Devols at last."

"I am certain we will. We are going to be more powerful than ever before."

"I hope you are right."

"With our powers combined, we might be stronger than the Devols."

"We owe it to Mohaba to do our best. If the Devols manage to save what might be protecting them, we are doomed." Mohabat's voice began to shake. She paused for a moment then sighed, "I wish we had done this earlier."

"Listen to me. We would have if we had known how."

"That is true, I know but …"

Buddha interrupted Mohabat, "I assure you we would have joined forces earlier if we had known Jewl kept them in power."

"We do know their weak spot now." Mohabat gained hope.

"That is right. Now we know their weakness. We have a great chance at defeating them. We must use it wisely."

"I have no doubts. I am ready to get started."

"Wonderful. You are a strong leader."

"Thank you, I promise my team will not let you down."

"I am delightful. I have a lot of practices in mind. You will not regret this. Just know your safety and identity will be my priority. You will be protected and that is my promise to you."

"Oh, does that mean we are not practicing with your students?"

"Not directly. But, in a way, we are all working together."

"What was I thinking? We, the Angelious, cannot be seen by your students."

"Exactly and there is no point in trying to reveal the Angelious to them."

Buddha and the Angelious warriors joined forces. I received reports from Buddha on how Mohabat and her group were doing. I observed their practices quite often. I could not help it. I had gotten used to watching my golden beauty. Now, the scene was different. It had a promising future.

Like the other warriors, Mohabat had no insights into her own heart and soul. All she understood was her destiny to fight the Devols. Her leadership skills and a strong sense of communication with Buddha impressed me. I had never thought much of her ability to fight. I watched her for centuries as a silent soul interacting with other Angelious. And although I had been concerned about the looming war, I worried equally about being reunited with the leader of the spiritual world whom I admired most.

Buddha quickly began taking his teachings to more challenging levels. Although under great pressure, he inspired those around him to remain strong. He engrained in his students his own determination and balance. He emphasized the importance of focusing, of staying in the present, to achieve internal peace. These were qualities that the Devols lacked.

What the Devols did not lack was the art of deception. We needed to remain focused to avoid their attempts to distract us from our goal. Although the Angelious were effective warriors, they were not connected to their own hearts and souls. Buddha recognized this weakness in their armor. He added a new training exercise designed to help the Angelious to focus on their inner souls.

Master Buddha began each afternoon's karate practice with yoga. At the beginning of each session, students were instructed to bring their hands close to their heart. They were then asked to take a deep breath and then, as they breathed out to utter one word, "ommmmmmm". With one breath, the voices of many harmonized into one powerful force. The resonance of the warriors' focus was extremely strong. It was so powerful that I had to create an invisible wall around the practice area to guard them against being detected. At the end of each lesson, the students again brought their hands close to their hearts, and, together, as one, they whispered the word, "Namaste." It is a word that was originated from Sanskrit meaning unity.

Some of the students were reluctant to take part in the yoga exercises. They did not recognize the importance of developing inner strength. But they had no choice. They always worked together as a team. It was something that Mohabat had taught them. Soon, the most reluctant warriors began to understand how their inner strength made them strong.

Buddha tracked the warrior's progress. I tried to give him my report at the end of each day before the warriors finished training. I used my special wooden bowl with its mirror water to observe them while away. I had discovered this bowl long ago with human Mohabat in the forest. Our Master did not have the luxury of time to track everyone's progress. I tried to help him as much as I could.

Disguised as a monk, except when alone with Mohabat and me, Buddha made us all believe we were stronger than the Devols. The power of that belief added strength. He had all of us gain faith despite our many years of failed attempts to defeat our enemy. Buddha reminded me when I looked skeptical, "With intense training, we will regain Mohaba's peace." I trusted his wisdom though I feared for Mohabat's safety. Like a parent, I wanted to protect her all the time.

Buddha selected the best monks, who could connect to the afterlife. He needed a strong team that could see the Devols in the forthcoming war. These monks had witnessed countless tragedies in Mohaba. Many times, they gave up their devout practices to save tortured babies, children, and wives, to help beaten husbands, victims of the Devols' cruelties. The monks had found their way to a nearby place filled with tortured survivors. Their leader, Buddha, helped the survivors of the Devol's brutality recover through intense yoga and meditation.

The survivors of the Devol's cruelty needed peace to recover. Buddha helped the victims to recover from their trauma before reuniting them with family. Some had come to believe their own families had betrayed them. Among the victims, Buddha discovered a group of gifted teenagers. It seemed that the trauma they suffered from the Devols blows to their heads, caused them to develop super powers. They could fly high up in the air while holding karate positions. After their recoveries, they became Mohaba's best karate fighters.

The student monks despised the Devols. They wanted to seek revenge. Some of them patiently waited for the day they would be welcomed back into their families. Until that day, they were engrossed in thoughts of destroying all the Devols. The monks could not see the Angelious, and only the senior monks who were trained by Buddha could see the Devols but not the Angelious. I disguised myself as a monk to help Buddha train the other students. While Buddha assisted the monks to develop inner strength, I enhanced their ability to identify the Devols.

In the meantime, the Devols made it impossible to view the mansion. They kept rapidly circling Jewl, blocking everyone's vision. Although we were preparing for a war, Buddha and I had no clear plans on to how we were going to proceed. We did not know what needed to be done to unlock the power of Jewl. We had no clue how much time we had to prevent the Devols to succeed at saving what they seemed to have been hiding. We were loath to waste one minute. Sadly, as spirits, we could not communicate with Mohaba's tortured residents. They had to remain in the dark about their possible release from the shackles the Devols had clamped on their town.

The Devols remained the strongest surviving evil force since the night of Mohabat's death. Over the centuries, they had proven more powerful than any other spirit forms. Now, we suspected through spreading rumors that their powers were directly connected to some precious spirits kept captive inside Jewl.

I began my search for the soul of Kerman's butler. After moving into his new home, Kerman noticed he needed an assistant to help run the household. He found a man right in Mohaba named Stephan who became a loyal butler. He took care of Kerman's family well until one day when he vanished without any clues or trace. I am uncertain how I missed his death. I have no recollection of his passing through the tunnel of re-birth. I hoped to find answers through his current life.

I paused in my duties to concentrate on finding Stephan's soul. I learned it now lived inside the mayor of a nearby town. I could not bear to kill the mayor to release his soul. I am not a killer; I take lives but award them life after death. If the butler's re-lived soul lived in an animal body, I would not have hesitated. I could not imagine taking his life before his time. He was a person with loved ones and responsibilities. Although the key to the Devol's extinction lay inside Jewl, I had to find another way to find answers.

The time to strike a war with the Devols seemed near. Kerman's decayed palace had become an easy target. All we had to do was find out what they were hiding in there that protected them all this time. I watched the warriors preparing for battle with the Devols. I knew that eventually, I would have to confront their leader. Although I knew how difficult it would be, I had to soon emerge from the shadows.

2

THE TEMPLES OF BANGKOK

Few days passed since the lightning that brought scourge of Devols to Jewl. Master Buddha instructed me to take his students to the temples of Bangkok. He felt confident about his their ability to spot the Devols. I had seen them wandering around the temples. We hoped, by visiting Bangkok, to find out not only the student's readiness but what Devols were up to.

I had not met Mohabat during our intense training days. I protected the practice area from the Devols. Our Master had spoken to Mohabat about me and my role as a protector. One day, I noticed Mohabat glanced at me while I had my back facing her. I had my monk robe on. I had no idea she would notice my scent. I disappeared before she tried to approach. Lots had unfolded since we had last met. I felt unprepared.

When Mohabat heard about Buddha's students going to Bangkok, she managed to approach me. I transformed back into a monk after going invisible. I detected her scent as she instantly neared. I fought hard to remain in control. All the countless years of waiting were about to end. I turned to face her.

We made eye contact. I could tell she was more nervous than me. Did she recognize something familiar, or nervous about approaching me? She asked me with her voice shaky, "Of all the great places for practice, why are you choosing Bangkok?" I could read curiosity on her face to see, me, Death, for the first time. I wanted to fully reveal myself. I hesitated as monks and warriors surrounded us. We needed privacy. I moved away from the group. Mohabat noticed that we needed to move away from the group so she followed me. All I could think of in that moment was how she had not said hello to me yet.

"Hello to you too, Mohabat." My decade of fear began to melt. She did not recognize me.

"How impolite of me. Hiiiieeeeyyy."

"Nice, so much better now." I grinned.

"Sorry, I totally forgot to say Hello. How impolite of me" Mohabat looked at me embarrassed. I could tell she felt tense.

"It is all right. We are all under a lot of pressure." I attempted to calm her down. I moved my gaze towards the practicing team.

"I know." Mohabat agreed. She brought my attention back to her.

"It is hard to tell what they are hiding inside Jewl."

"Even I cannot see inside there."

"They are powerful, indeed."

"There is so much at stake this time. We have to act fast." I unconsciously mentioned this time. Then, I recalled Mohabat does not remember our past. She has no memory. I did not try to correct myself and bring her attention to it. I let her carry on the conversation. Luckily, she did not notice.

"We have no idea who we are fighting against," Mohabat stated furiously.

"Yes, we do. But, we have to be wise about it." I glimpsed back at the team for a short moment.

"Buddha has told me so much about you and your involvement."

"I understand he has." I did not know what Mohabat planned to ask me next.

"I heard you are going to the temples. You did not tell me why?"

"Right, Bangkok, why?"

"Yes, why there?" Mohabat asked with wonder.

"I know there are some Devols lurking there."

"Oh, really, why you think …?"

I interrupted her, anticipating her question, "I suspect they are up to something. I am quite sure, actually." I tried my best to stay in character, to maintain the charade. I felt old recalling the last time we were in contact. I had disguised myself as a young monk. I had similar features to the Mahboo she had known before. I turned my voice into a young man, someone her age. My real voice would have scared her with its ugliness.

"Are you sure it is safe to go if Devols are there?" Mohabat asked. She seemed concerned for my safety. Nonetheless, puzzled by her concern for someone she barely knew.

I became distracted, sensing a strong connection to Mohabat. I hoped to bring my focus back to our conversation. "Well, first, I have to visit Buddha's students, whom he has ranked as the ablest to overthrow Devols."

"I see, and ..." Mohabat uttered in an assertive voice just like a strong leader.

"And ..." I paused in thought. I gazed at the forest hoping to distract myself from Mohabat's beauty. I could smell her old familiar human odor before she died. I no longer felt any parental connection to her. She had grown into an immortal mature woman. The distance between us seemed to have washed away any confusion I had about my true feelings for her.

I planned to cut our conversation short. I wanted the looming battle to disappear first. I composed myself. "I am detecting students who are not ready. We will not take them with us to Bangkok." I looked towards the fighting team thereby avoiding Mohabat's eyes. I worried she would recognize me and our past.

"You did not answer the question of its safety." Mohabat no longer seemed nervous. Her words brought my attention back to her face. Her big brown eyes stared deep into my eyes.

"Yes, it is safe." I leaned on a nearby tree. Mohabat moved beside me. She could sense my wavering attention. In fact, I distracted myself by focusing on the unseen wall I had created to protect the students from the Devols.

"How do you know that? No one has ever survived being around the Devols."

"Do not worry."

"I cannot help but to be worried."

"I can disguise myself into any shape I want. Devols cannot detect me unless I decide to reveal myself, which will not happen."

"Is that enough? What about the student's safety?"

"I will not let them out of my sight." Again, I moved my gaze back towards the practicing team.

"Alright, if you say so. Why do I not have the same powers you have?" Mohabat prodded. She knew the answer. I could tell she wanted to keep the conversation going. She could not explain why she was drawn to me. After all, I could destroy her. I could take her soul away at any time.

I answered her attentively. "I am designed for it. This is what I do."

"I see."

"The thing is when the body is giving up its soul, I can take it over instantly."

"You can do that?"

"Yes. I cannot behave like that person, though. Not that easy."

"I bet."

"If you were Death, I am sure you would have had this ability."

"But, I am not." Mohabat sounded envious.

"But, I know for a fact there is only one Death on this planet and that is me."

"It must be nice. I only know I am a skilled warrior."

"A great one."

"I am curious as to how you manage your powers over life and death?"

"Tough one."

"I bet it must be tiring."

I tried to describe myself to Mohabat, "I am the only one in charge of taking lives. The universal gods order me when, and where to direct the soul as it is released."

"You know, I pictured you as a frightening man desperately craving for blood. Hmmm, perhaps I was not accurate."

"Do not worry. I am used to it. You are not the first one to think this way. If I could reveal myself as otherwise, I would."

"That can never happen, can it? I mean, you would not be able to do what you do if they saw you, right." I saw Mohabat almost smile. "I did not imagine you as a good person, you know."

"That's OK. I like to think of myself as siding with Good. I feel close to the gods."

"Me too."

"Maybe I feel this way because the universe chose me to carry out its wishes."

"It seems we all have our own destined parts to play."

"Yes, my role, sadly, does come with a great sense of responsibility."

"I can only imagine."

"It is exhausting, I must add."

Mohabat admired, "I wish I felt close to the universal gods the way you do. I believe there is a higher power. I try to believe in them but you know what …"

"What?"

Mohabat paused, staring into my eyes. "My God might be different from yours."

"You think so?"

"I have phases. There are days that I am hopeful the gods will help bring Mohaba back to its golden days. I heard it from the tree souls how beautiful our town used to be."

"You did?" I asked although I knew.

Mohabat nodded, "Yes, but I have no recollection of it. I can only picture … it is difficult for me. I have no memories whatsoever. I believe them. I must admit I envy you." For a moment, we both silently watched the monks going through their drills.

I convinced Mohabat, "We all have a destiny. You do too."

"I know we do."

"As Death, I have been able to get rid of many evil beings."

Mohabat, excited, interrupted me, "I have prepared my team to do the same. We have an eye for the forest. We sometimes battle evil forms. Sadly, we have been rather unsuc-cessful with the Devols, only them."

"We will outsmart them." I heartedly stated.

"I fear Devols have been spreading throughout the entire galaxy."

"They may have by now."

"We have to stop them before they take over," I stressed loudly.

"I hope Jewl holds the answer. These Devols are ruthless but definitely not intelligent."

"That is true; they do not focus on anything for long. They may have a lot of powers but no brains."

"We will show them. You have the help of all my warrior talents."

"That is great. You are positive … sending this good energy to your team." I brought my focus back on the monks, who could not see the warriors wandering around my guarded protective wall. The warriors could see the monks but the students could not see the Angelious practicing karate in the air.

"You do not mind me asking you this …" Mohabat said, puzzled.

"I do not mind, go ahead."

"Do you believe if you risked revealing yourself to Devols, you may have been able to save Mohaba sooner?"

"Hmmm …"

"I am terribly sorry. What was I thinking? I should not have asked."

"You have asked me a tough question. I am aware of the Devols' existence. I know how contagious it has been."

"I am sorry, I did not mean to ... You do not have to answer if you do not want to ..."

I interrupted Mohabat, "It is all right. You have to understand the reason I have not done anything until now is my responsibility."

"I understand. I was curious, that is all."

"I am the only Death. If there were other versions of me somewhere, maybe I would risk it."

We watched Buddha approaching. He looked directly at me as he spoke, not wanting the monks to sense Mohabat's presence. "How are you both? It looks like you are in the middle of a serious conversation. Has Mahboo told you about his special powers yet?"

Mohabat smiled, "Not yet."

"Alright, I will leave you two alone."

Mohabat grinned, "Thank you Master."

"You are welcome." Buddha looked at Mohabat, then turned his head towards me. "Mahboo, make sure she knows, we do not have much time." Buddha walked back to his students and soon busied himself explaining the intricacies of a particularly effective fighting strategy.

I looked back to Mohabat. "Where were we?"

"I think you were telling me about your death duties."

"That is right. I need to inform you of what I can do."

"What do you do exactly when someone dies?"

"What do I do? Well, now a living creature dies, I assign

its soul to its next life form if I can. I am now able to do this mostly without any need to be present."

Mohabat interestedly asks me, "For how long have you been Death? Is it something that you were born with or awarded with?"

"Good question. I have been working since the beginning of time. I have had no birth. I did not grow. I opened my eyes to a planet ready to have living creatures."

"It is no surprise then, it has become a habit for you, spontaneously taking lives. You must have learned to adapt perfectly to your circumstances. This is beyond extraordinary."

"I am not sure if you can call it extraordinary. It is more a responsibility. I could abandon it if I wanted to, but then, that would mean that the world that I love would end." I had to make sure Mohabat knew why I had not risked my cover to save Mohaba. I explained to her, "When Devols took over Mohaba, I had no other choice but to carry on with my obligation as the one and only, you know. I got placed in an uncomfortable situation."

"I totally understand, you do not need to go further with that."

I carried on, "I did not know for quite some time how to destroy these terrible creatures. I would have, but ..." I paused realizing Mohabat had been carefully listening to every word I uttered.

"Go on ..."

I voiced, "I do not know what Devols would do if they

found out about me. The worst scenario is that if I were elim-inated, the entire world would end."

"You do not need to explain further."

"I feel like I do."

"I think now that I know more about your abilities; I have a better understanding of why you could not risk it all."

"There must be a reason you asked."

"You were protecting us. I understand. Really," she spoke with passion in her eyes while gazing deeply into my eyes.

"I am glad you do. From now on, things are going to be different. With the Devol's secret place revealed, at last, I am hopeful."

Mohabat confident, "I am too, Mahboo. That is your name, am I right? Mahboo? I heard Buddha call you by that name."

"Yes, it is. You know, I am willing to risk everything to destroy them forever. I mean it when I say forever and ever …"

Mohabat giggled at my comment. "And ever and ever, here." Both of us laughed with relief. We strongly believed we could defeat the Devols. I changed the subject. "As you can see, I am muscular because of the number of souls I have to carry each day. I have extremely dark features …"

Mohabat interrupted, "Yes, I noticed. Let me guess, to pro-tect you from being seen."

"Even if someone sees me, and they have, they do not understand exactly what it is they are seeing. Many have thought I was a demon or that they had lost their mind."

We both laughed again. Our conversation switched from

serious to funny. Mohabat's fear of me melted. She admitted softly as she stared into my eyes, "You are right. You have such black hair and eyes. There is no light traveling in them."

She flattered me. "As you can see, my gown is also quite dark, almost invisible, looks nothing like what has been written in the papers about me."

"They have no clue about you. You have done a great job not being discovered."

"I guess, I have no accessories, only this gown, which makes me invisible to any spirit wandering around. That might explain why."

"I wish I could do that. It would have been nice if I could vanish and the warriors could not see me." Mohabat giggled.

"Well, I can if you like, turn you invisible. You can see what it is like to be me. I can fit you inside."

Mohabat amazed, "I must say, I think that is the greatest gift one can have."

Still flattered, I continued, "I do not just have invisibility powers. I am able to take charge of the souls of the dying and reincarnate them."

"This is absolutely amazing. You are telling me about another world that I doubted ever existed. It is magical. My head is spinning thinking about it."

"Well, easier said than done."

"Sorry, go on." Distracted Mohabat attempted to look serious.

Her enthusiasm urged me on. "I can take any being's soul.

I can throw it into my violin-like tunnel. It is my secret garden. I call it 'Behesht'. I reincarnate them there."

"Behesht, what a beautiful word. It sounds so peaceful. Sorry, do go on."

"To decide how the soul will appear in its next reincarnation, I have to sometimes touch the forehead of the dying creature."

"What happens when you do that?"

"Their life is played back to me in a flash. I can then decide where to direct the soul for its subsequent rebirth."

"That is incredible. I must call you the Master of life and death from now on."

"Thank you. I think it is fair to say that I have mastered the circle of life. At least, I like to think so. I run it as if I am running a factory."

"Why is that?"

"That is because it now runs itself almost without my presence." I paused for a moment. I then noticed Mohabat is mesmerized to hear all about me.

"That sounds almost unreal."

I felt rushed to tell her everything she needed to know. Buddha demanded me to familiarize her with my abilities. He found it necessary since we were going to work together in this battle. I began to hurry my words, "As you can guess by now, my place on the planet helps the process of death and rebirth to run without me."

"I bet."

"I do not constantly need to be in the beds of a dying."

"I bet the invisible gods play a part in helping you with this." Mohabat increased her attention.

"Maybe. It could be. It is handy that I do not consciously decide the deceased's next life."

"I mean if not then …"

"Well, I had to do it for such a long that it is automatic to me. That might be why. But, you could be right. The gods might have a part in this."

"Otherwise, it almost sounds impossible."

"If it so, then maybe they work through me."

"Right."

"Over time, I figured out an efficient way of handling the increased population of the world, with people dying every instant."

"You must have mastered it over time."

"I cannot quite tell. I like to think I have."

"You sure have. You basically run the world." Mohabat remained attentive.

"To be honest, it is more a duty to me than anything else."

Mohabat with conviction, "You are the reason we all exist, that there is life on this planet."

"Well, it is my duty to make sure it stays safe." I began feeling the need to rush our talk again. Our conversation seemed to take longer than I anticipated.

"Well, you are guarding the world. You are also keeping the world safe by keeping holy souls like Buddha's alive." Mohabat mentioned as she moved her look towards the disguised Buddha. She went into a moment of deep thoughts. Her curiosity impressed me.

I speeded my talk. "Well, to be honest with you, it is hard for me to say if I have power over that decision or whether the gods of the universe are the ones who award immortality through me, their surrogate."

"Regardless, you are keeping our world safe. That is what matters, in the end, Mahboo. You are putting yourself last and the people first. It is honorable."

I felt Mohabat's admiration. However, I knew we could not carry on our conversation in the slow pace that it was moving. We had plenty of time after the battle to have talks like these. Buddha had instructed me to tell Mohabat all my powers. That would be the only way I could help to protect her. However, we were running out of time. I had plans to meet with Buddha's students before heading to Bangkok. I hurried to finish. "Oh, um, thank you. It means a lot to hear you say these nice words to me. I try." Then, I hurried back to tell her about my other abilities, "Anyhow, I would like you to know and this is something no one knows, not even our Master. I can jump into and become a body before it is dead."

"Really, how?"

"I do it before the blood and heart have stopped. It is not easy because I must return the body back after. It is complicated. I only do it if I have to." I hoped to end the conversation at this point. We had been talking for over an hour. I enjoyed our talk but also found it difficult to stand beside a woman who meant the world to me.

Mohabat frowned, deep in thought. "If you are using the body for the right reasons, I see nothing wrong with that. I am sure the universal gods probably gave you this ability to be used for good deeds."

"Honestly, I am not sure if I am permitted or not. I have never met them you know. I sense their presence sometimes but that is all. I guess you could say they work through me. Good or bad, I am not sure. I do not question it."

"I feel the same way. I have never seen the gods myself or the god that I like to believe in. They are invisible and undetectable which makes me question if it is true that they exist. I am not sure if it is their voice constantly playing in my head or my own. I cannot tell."

I detected warmth emanating from Mohabat. Up till now, she seemed to be making conversation with an interesting acquaintance. I could now sense she felt this strong connection with someone she barely knew and could not understand why. No one else in her group had ever made her feel butterflies in her stomach like she felt in my presence.

I felt proud to hold a real conversation with Mohabat. I responded, "I am not sure either. I do feel some higher presence around me at times. I guess that is good enough."

"You either believe in them or do not. I think both you and I do, I feel their presence at times. It does not matter that I have not seen them with my own eyes."

"It is true. To be honest, most of the burden is on me. It is not funny to play with people's souls. It is not easy. You have no idea how tiring it can be."

"I can only imagine."

"If I do have to use a body temporarily then I have to return it later to the scene of the accident and cover up all my tracks. It does not always feel right." After a pause, I whispered to Mohabat, revealing some of my grief, "I do not have DNA. I guess I will not get caught."

"That is incredible."

"But it is exhausting. Trust me, you would not want to be me."

"I understand you, Mahboo. I know you would not do any of it for pleasure. That is for sure."

"I try but you know, half the time, I question not only myself, but this world."

Mohabat paused for a second. She then changed the topic while insisting, "Tell me more about why you are going to Bangkok?"

"Buddha has selected the students whom he is convinced are ready for battle in Jewl."

"Well, that is wonderful, is it not?"

"Hmmm, some of these students have been abused by the Devols. Devols did the crimes, not them, even though their families think they did." I grieved as I had for years for these innocent victims.

Mohabat sighed, "I know. I see it happening. I sometimes do not believe my own eyes."

"The Devols' victims want their justice just as badly as they want to prove to their innocence to their families."

"I cannot believe these monsters."

"You know, for some of the students, fighting Devols will be their best medicine. It will make them stronger. They will leave the abuse behind. But for others, facing the Devols will weaken them."

"I know. I see and watch them from far, it is pretty sad."

"And the only way to know which way each student will react is to shake their hand. That is why I am introducing myself as Buddha's most powerful monk."

Mohabat appeared surprised. "Is it necessary for you to shake their hands? Won't they sense something from you?"

"Possibly, but it is a risk I must take."

Just when I felt proud of myself for having made it this far without giving myself away, Mohabat asked, "Will you please take me with you? I know it might be hard since some of them might see me now, but please, let me go with you. I am willing to risk my cover."

"Hmmm, I am not sure." I knew the answer to Mohabat's question. I pretended that I needed a moment to think. I tried not to let my feelings for her influence my decision. I answered, "I do not think they are trained to see any Ange-lious. Buddha does not think they can but it is better to be safe than sorry, right? And honestly, I am not sure if I am per-mitted to." Then, without thinking, words uttered out of me, "But I could take you if you are hidden under my gown. I do not think anyone will know."

"I will not be seen at all that way?"

"Well, it is risky."

"I see nothing wrong with it. We are doing this in preparation for a tough battle ahead. It is for a good cause, is it not? Will you, please … please take me with you, Mahboo? There is so much to learn from this experience. I might be of help."

"Alright, I can take you with me. We are breaking the rules. And if you disappear for long, there is a risk that you will vanish for good."

"I am willing to take the risk. I have a feeling there is much to learn from this."

"You know Mohabat, you may never come back. You do not want that, now do you?" I was reminded of when she used to be a child, negotiating for a favor as I resisted her pleading.

"I trust that you will make sure I will not disappear. It is just a test anyway … it is not going to take long, or will it?"

"We could be there for several hours. I have never tried it for that long." I lied.

"This is going to be so much fun. I have not had much fun in a long time."

"Yes, but remember, we are not doing this for enjoyment."

"I know, but Mahboo, you know we owe it to ourselves to have a little excitement. You do not think it is good for the soul?"

"You are funny, I like that."

"Will you take me then?" Mohabat's eyes widened as she brought her face close to mine.

I could never say no to Mohabat when she did that. I became overwhelmed with excitement to be near her again.

"We have to test it out first. My gown is designed to hold only me for any length of time."

"I understand."

"It can only conceal an additional soul for a short time, exactly how long, I do not know." I strained to sound nonchalant. "Alright, we can try it now and see. If I cannot do it then I cannot take you with me. Deal?"

Mohabat's face broke into a smirk. She replied with confidence, "Deal."

I know exactly my threshold. I did not want to make Mohabat get used to these whole non-existent fun games. It could become irresistibly addictive.

"I am ready when you are." Cheerful Mohabat uttered while standing up, looking at me for direction.

"Please hold my hand tight. Ready? Here, hang on to my back. Good, now try to hug me from behind. Do not be scared. I will carry your weight."

Mohabat gazed into my eyes. I started to feel almost whole again. I pulled her near. I wrapped my gown around her like a blanket. She slowly disappeared although able to feel, see and hear. She hugged me tightly. I carried her as if there was no extra weight on me. Mohabat was almost tempted to go with me over to where her Angelious friends were to see what they were up to, I reminded her of our limited time.

I worried of the dangers to keeping Mohabat invisible. After all, I could unconsciously draw her soul out of her body. After testing out our abilities together, it became almost time to go to Bangkok. I needed to stop by Buddha's cave to go over our plans. I dropped Mohabat off close to her home in the forests. We arranged to meet back near the House of Temples after sunset.

3

BEFORE NIGHT FALL IN BANGKOK

Before sundown, I visited Buddha in his cave. Master and I needed to identify students whom we believed had been weakened by their traumas at the hands of Devols. Both Master and I were aware that the student monks could see the Devols. But this did not guarantee their strength to handle them. After touching up my disguise, Buddha asked me, "Mahboo, are you certain that you are ready for this task?" I identified genuine concern in Buddha's voice.

"I think I am."

"Are you certain?"

"Yes, I have been trying for a long time to find out how to defeat them. I am as ready as I can be." I watched Buddha, reading there was more to his question than the danger of facing our enemy.

"You do understand that it is not all about you. This is for a higher cause—Mohaba's tortured, neighbors and victims."

"I do understand, Master."

"Good. Then, we need to find out which one of my students might need to be taken out of their team."

I knew this would be a tough decision but said nothing. Master concerned, "Mahboo. You cannot let your emotions distract you. I know you learned it from raising Mohabat long ago."

"I did. I know. Before I met her, I was emotionless. Now, I possess human traits that I did not believe existed in me."

"True, I do understand and feel you, Mahboo. But, we are here to put together the strongest battle-ready team, this moment, to help us destroy the demons that torture us all." Buddha gazed directly into my eyes, "We must use our mind's eye. That is the only way to stop the abuse from continuing any longer."

"I fully understand."

"Therefore, we will be helping the students accomplish just that, whether they feel ready."

"It is important."

"We are going to eliminate their enemy. You realize then Mahboo …?"

I placed my right hand on Buddha's left shoulder. I looked directly into his eyes, "I really do. I am your believer."

"Good. Now, there is another matter I feel strongly we need to discuss before we go on."

"I am listening." I took my hand from his shoulder to show I was paying attention.

"Actually, I think you do know what I am about to say."

Our conversation took another turn. "Oh, of course. Mohabat?"

"Yes, Mohabat. I understand you ..."

"Master, please, you need to say no more. I will not take her with me to Bangkok."

"No, actually I do want you to take her with you. That is not the problem."

"Really, then what is it?"

"I can see you have put a limit on her."

"I have."

"I need to warn you on another matter... so you can be prepared." Master's face turned stern.

I feared what Buddha was going to say next. I preempted him, "I will not let my feelings get in the way. I promise you that."

"Mahboo, it is clearly too late. You are in love with Mohabat."

"What I mean is, I do not plan on making the same mistakes again."

"I know you do not."

"I am much stronger now than I used to be. The distance between us has helped. It is for her good. I must stay out of her personal life."

"We need, to be honest. You have in some way."

"It is out of care."

"If it was only care, you would have said no when she begged to come to Bangkok with you." Buddha took a deep breath. He then questioned me, "Are you ever able to say no to Mohabat?"

"True, no. I am afraid I cannot."

"Then, it is not only feelings of care, now is it?"

"Alright, I love her the same and maybe more. But I am not going to allow myself to fall in love with her again."

"Easier said than done, is it not, Mahboo?"

"I am serious. I made up my mind long ago. That is why I have stayed out of her way all these years. You know that well."

"Mahboo, listen. I am not against love. Not for mankind nor for those in kind healthy loving relationships. I am all for love and peace. You know that about me."

"I do. That is why I look up to you as much as I look up to our gods. I know you truly want what is best for both her and me. There is no doubt in my mind."

"You are going to spend some time with her over the rooftops of these beautiful Temples."

"That is true."

"Well, I hope you take what I have to say to heart."

"I will try. You can count on my word."

Buddha became firm. He asserted, "You cannot and I mean it, Mahboo, you cannot tell Mohabat about the tragedy of her past."

"It is hard not to."

Master repeated, "You cannot tell her about her tragic past." His tone softened, "I know it is hard."

I sighed, "It is."

"She will ask you many times while she is gazing into your eyes with her golden beauty, tempting you to give in. You have to make sure you do not tell her yet, OK Mahboo?"

"But … I cannot lie. Especially to those whom I care deeply for." I paused with a sigh and bared, "If I lied to her when she was human … she would not have chosen to help me. I put her in danger. I could not lie about what I do."

"I understand. You will not be lying to her, Mahboo. OK? Withholding the truth is not considered a lie, my friend."

"If she asks me, how do I withhold the truth?"

"You see Mahboo, a lie is when you say something that is far from the truth. You are actually going, to be honest with her."

"I am?"

"Yes, you will convince her that it is in her best interest that she is not told about her past all at once."

"I see."

"That is all. Can you do that?"

"I think she deserves to know everything. I am in contact with her again after all this time. Postponing telling her the truth would mean that I am intentionally keeping a secret about her past. I want a clean start with her."

"Mahboo, you have to trust me. If you tell her, she will

be no different from our students who are unable to move beyond their experiences at the hands of the Devols."

"She will not be. I know her. She is different."

"We have no time for that. Right now, we need her to focus on becoming stronger for the battle. We need her." Buddha held my gaze.

"You are advising me not tell her since, in your opinion, it could interfere with her ability to fight. Am I correct?"

"Yes."

"She will be told though just not right now."

"Yes, exactly, not right now. This is for the best. Hang in there just a little bit longer. Will you, Mahboo?"

"Alright."

"And when the time is right, you have to be careful how you tell her. Never forget; information is power."

"I definitely know that from observing humans."

"We do not want her to go into battle with any doubts or resentments. We need her strength."

I walked towards the image Buddha scratched on the ground with his sword. I thought about the situation. I stared at the image of the woman sitting in a yoga pose. "This is not going to be easy for me. It will be harder when I must break the news to her later. Mohabat will wonder why I lied to her."

Buddha felt my pain. He sighed but promised, "I will be here to help you whenever you need me."

"Thank you. So, it is definitely all right if I take her?"

"Absolutely. This will be a good test for both of you."

"I hope."

"First, figure out if you have the strength to carry her for that long." Buddha grinned.

"I think I can handle it although it has been a while since I have done it." I grinned back.

"Alright then." Buddha transformed into a monk.

"Well then." I began to prepare psychologically for the task ahead. "I like the name Jadoo. What do you think?"

"Yes, that name will do. We will do anything for our universe and its people, right Mahboo? Oh, sorry, Jadoo. Right," Buddha grinned again.

I felt confident that we reached an agreement. "Right, Master Ghavi." I called him the name by which he was known to his students.

"Now, we have some work to do before you and Mohabat head to Bangkok, do we not?"

I nodded my head, "That is true."

"Shall we go shake some hands?"

We returned to the practice area. Buddha grabbed everyone's attention. "Please listen." All the students turned their heads towards Buddha and me. Ghavi asserted with a rising voice, "I would like to introduce you to the strongest and most-skilled member of our group."

I could hear some of the students whispering to each other that they did not know the reason for my presence. Master continued, "I want to make sure that you are ready, that you know exactly what your practice lesson will be. If anyone wishes not to go, please tell me now." Master waited. He did not wish his students to have any fears. The Devols smelled fear. If the Devols discovered them through their fears, there would be no battling monks left except Buddha himself. Master Ghavi decided to send all his students to the House of Temples.

Buddha prepared himself for the difficult task of telling some of his students that they would not be allowed to go with the rest of the team. He anticipated that none of the students would confess that they were scared or unprepared, or that some might not know how unprepared they were. I began shaking each student's hand. I shook the hand of each of the first five students and felt the strength and commitment of a warrior. But as soon as I made eye contact with the sixth student, a young man named, Badoo, I felt a warning tremor, as if from a distant earthquake. I removed my hand and nodded discreetly at Buddha, who knew exactly what had to be done.

"Thank you, Jadoo for taking our students on this challenging expedition."

"It is my pleasure, Master."

"You are one of our strongest monks. You have a clear vision for the Devols. I understand you are going to test our students on their response to the presence of the Devols?"

I looked at all the students standing in front of me. They all gazed directly at me. "Yes, we are."

I shared with them, "It is going to be a dangerous assignment. I believe in every one of you. I can see you are ready."

Buddha called to the sixth student whose touch sent tremors through the air, "Badoo, please come here. I need to talk to you for a second." He agreed. Ghavi whispered to Badoo, "I need you to stay here with me and help me with something."

Badoo became visibly upset. He lowered his voice. "But Master, I thought we were all going. How am I going to know if I can see the Devols if I am not given a chance like everyone else?"

"Badoo. I am terribly sorry. You are not ready."

"How can you know for sure Master Ghavi?"

"You need more practice time. Be patient, my son. These demons are extremely strong. Do you want to risk falling into the hands of the Devols again?"

"Of course, not, Master. If you believe I am not ready, then let me be of help to you in other ways. If we get rid of these Devols, then I will be happy. Rest assured. Will you still let me practice, please?"

"Yes, I will. I may not take you to Jewl."

Badoo agreed, "I understand. Will you please help me become ready? I know I can do this"

"Alright, Badoo but no promises, OK?"

"Agreed. Thank you. Thank you so much."

"Promise me you will be OK if we end up not taking you with us?"

Badoo pretended to agree but insisted, "Yes, but … but at least, I will know I tried. Do I not deserve a second chance, Master?"

"Yes, yes you do my son. No doubt. We need to go and pray for our teammates to return home safely."

Master Ghavi put his arm around Badoo, proud of his determination, and took him to a quiet place to meditate. They prayed for those precious to them. Badoo prayed for the people of Mohaba, especially his family whom he missed dearly. Ever since the day he killed his own sister, while possessed by a Devol, he was ashamed to go home. He was given the honor of joining the monks' community, which helped him get through his unbearable guilt. Buddha, repeatedly, prayed for his students, Mohabat and me. If any of us failed, we would be revealed to the Devols, thereby putting everything that we worked hard for in jeopardy.

4

THE NIGHT IN BANGKOK

I met Mohabat close to House of Temples. The moon buried behind a curtain of black clouds. I hid Mohabat under my gown and, disguised as Jadoo, joined the students. As we approached the Temples, I instructed the students to continue without me. "I will be up on the roof. If I see any of you in danger, I will deal with it. Stay calm. I will not let these monsters harm you. Try to hold still when in fear. Is everyone ready? If you have questions, ask now."

In a group, "No Jadoo, we are ready."

"Good. Remember. Act like any other monk ready to pray."

Mohabat and I headed to the roofs. I used my karate skills to climb up while Mohabat stayed hidden underneath my cloak. We reached the top. We gazed down into the courtyard and immediately spotted Devols. We locked our gaze towards the student monks. Mohabat and I began to whisper to each other. The cloak protected our voices.

"Oh, my Mahboo. How do you do this? I feared they would see me."

"This is good practice. When we go to battle, there may be times you have to travel this way with me."

"It is something to get used to. You must teach me how to keep up with your speed and movements. Do not forget."

"You are doing well."

Mohabat lowered her tone to near muttering. "Thank you. It is nice to have someone believe in me for once."

"I am glad."

"With my team, I find I have to prove myself to them all the time. It is tiring."

"I have no doubt that it is."

"Do not look at my thick skin. It is soft inside."

I did not say another word. I admired the woman my baby girl had become. I took her gentle, inviting hand in mine. Mohabat did not pull away. It felt like the old days except that she was no longer human. The moment felt like a magical salve for my wounds. I detected Mohabat's heart warm up. I could hear it almost beating. I could tell she was comfortable near me. I prayed having her this close to me would not bring her memory back or it would threaten our victory.

Mohabat sighed, "Oh Mahboo, I wish I could feel my heartbeat. I wish I had love, the kind that humans have. I do not know what it is like to be loved. Maybe if I was human …"

"Why human?" I wondered. I had no contact with Mohabat since she became an Angelious.

Her innocent curiosity reflected in her face. "I long to experience how humans feel."

"Sometimes, it is better not to be human," I said without looking at Mohabat. I had my eyes glued on our masked monks.

"Well, I am not so sure."

"Look at what Mohaba's people are going through. So much torture. So much suffering. Yes, there is love in between all that but it comes with the price of pain. You are free. You can do what pleases you. You do not see the boundless beauty of what you have?"

"I do."

"What if your family suffered torture? How would you feel?"

"I know, I know, Mahboo. It is an innocent curiosity. That is all."

"You can distance yourself from the pain you feel my dear, but they cannot." I hoped to convince Mohabat. I endured the pain of her not living her destiny. I am not human but raising Mohabat woke human emotions in me that has stayed with me ever since she died. Her unrecalled human life was short. I hid my regret.

Mohabat distracted, moves her gaze away from the courtyard. She looks at me, convinced, "It is true, but they get to feel emotions and love much more deeply than I ever can." Maybe inside her soul, Mohabat felt incomplete. She never had a chance to live a full life.

"Who said you cannot feel? If you feel your heartbeat, you can feel love, maybe more so than humans." I glimpsed at Mohabat but turned my look back down at the ground tracking every move the students made.

"You do not know that."

The students seemed to be all right. They walked in separate areas near different temples. I had to pay close attention. Our view was blocked when they walked pass the big temples. I barely heard the last words Mohabat uttered to me. I momentarily brought my attention back to her. "Go on, I am listening," I said, with my eyes glued to the students.

"I am frustrated. I want to know who I was before I died."

"I know," I sighed.

"What is wrong? Tell me, is it about my past, is it?"

"Yes."

"But, it is so long ago. Wait a minute. You are Death. You took my life. You do know, don't you?"

"Yes, I do." I froze, my guilt began to overwhelm me.

Mohabat shocked, "I cannot believe I did not guess earlier."

"Um, how do I say this without … the truth is, hmm," I looked down at the student monks. They seemed fine. The Devols did not suspect their presence in the courtyard. I did not know what to say to Mohabat. All the centuries of keeping it in had taken their toll. The relief was immense, which explained why I could not think of how to respond to my girl.

"Oh, are you all right?"

I moved Mohabat's hands away. "I … hmmm …" I recalled Buddha's words. I paused for a second, remembering my promise to him. I stopped talking altogether.

Mohabat's voice rose, "Mahboo, do not stop. I need to know." Her voice slowly softened, "Do not stop now. Look, the students all seem fine."

"Alright, all right but we cannot take our eyes off them. Where do I begin? Hauhhhhh hmmm …"

"Anywhere."

"Something about you. I could tell from the moment I found you that you were quite different from the rest of the women in Mohaba. You possessed a soul that no other human being ever did."

"Go on."

"You looked then just as you do now. Have you ever noticed you are different from all the other Angelious?"

Mohabat tried to keep her voice down, "No, I have not. How am I really?"

"That is because, my darling, you cannot see your soul. In special moments, when you are fully happy, you glow."

"Really, I glow? How?"

"You possess the heart of a golden spirit. If you come to recognize it, it is there. There are no other angelic spirits in the world as highly ranked."

Mohabat tried to keep her emotions under control. "I do

not understand what makes me different from my team. I have worked hard for many centuries to become a leader. I have earned my place."

"No, no, I do not mean … you have. I know you have earned your leadership. Anyway, you will discover why soon."

I had been given another chance to make things right. I had many confessions that I needed to make to Mohabat. I missed having her close to me. No matter how hard it seemed at times, I would remain faithful to the gods of the universe, to myself, to the Mohabat of my memories and to the Angelious Mohabat.

Ever since Mohabat had come into my world, I developed a human curiosity about things around me. Admiring Mohabat fulfilled my selfish need to be close to something pure. She is fresh, like fresh blood, protected within the body, alive with oxygen. She is the opposite of me, I am the blood that dries and blackens once it leaves the body.

I absorbed my thoughts and returned to the original plan suggested by Master. He advised me to dish out any fragments of the story to Mohabat. I repeatedly reminded myself of Master's advice, "Mahboo, come on, focus on what is at hand. Winning Mohabat over or saving Mohaba? You will have both after the battle ends. Breathe deeply whenever in doubt. Once done, you will think more clearly."

The Devol's attack on Jewl had brought Mohabat back into my life. We were working for the universal gods together now. We were helping to save not only Mohaba, but the whole universe. The stakes were high. If we won, peace and prosperity would return to Mohaba and possibly our entire planet. If we lost, the situation would be worse than before. With our defeat, Devols would most likely possess the entire universe. They remained in Mohaba for many centuries. I worried that they had bigger plans to destroy our planet if not the universe itself.

I knew Buddha had been right. We had to focus on preparing for the war. Unlike me, at least Mohabat had not been left with any tragic memories. I had to live with the pain for centuries while she lived with no painful thoughts. I stopped my disruptive thoughts and brought my focus back on concentrating on the positive stories. I briefly told Mohabat the extraordinary story of her birth. The students had successfully fooled the Devols that they were real monks. No drop of suspicion was raised by the Devols. The right time had come for me to let her know. I remained cautious. I started tenderly, "I will tell you why I love you."

"Love me?"

"It is because I raised you."

"What? This cannot be true, can it?" Mohabat's voice tightened. She could hardly breathe.

"Try to breathe. Relax, my dear. Once you hear everything, it all will make sense."

Mohabat's tone tensed, "You are not my father. It does not make sense ... I mean. This is not possible. You are Death. I would have been Death too, wouldn't I?"

"I raised you. I watched you grow into the beautiful

woman that you did, I mean, that you have." I stared into Mohabat's eyes. Her eyes tensed up. Luckily, I had a reason to look away. I brought my focus back to the yard full of temples and praying monks. I watched the students below to avoid looking in Mohabat's angry face. "No, listen … you wanted to know who you are. Let me explain to you from the beginning, at least."

Mohabat, calmed. "I am listening. I have been waiting centuries for this moment. My ears are all yours."

I looked back at her, "Good, it does not hurt, does it?"

She almost laughed. Her voice softened, "Not really." Mohabat relaxed. She moved her gaze towards the yard as she prepared to listen.

But before I could begin, a shout interrupted us. In an instant, Mohabat retreated under my cloak. I transformed back into Jadoo. We crept down to the courtyard. The monks were flustered. Apparently, a Devol managed to steal the soul of one of the golden statues. I gathered the monks together and instructed the students to leave the temple immediately. They were not fully ready to fight the Devols. The monks understood but the students were upset. They had no chance to test their abilities to spot the Devols. I called out to Master Ghavi to come and take the students somewhere safe.

After the students left, I turned to the Devols. I wanted to show Mohabat how well I could fight. I picked up two wooden sticks. I approached the two Devols. They each moved into a fighting stance, brandishing their sticks, and the fight began. First, I attacked using Lerdrit. The Muay Thai fight that we began was nothing near ordinary.

The two Devols responded to my attack. I turned their weapons to dust. I drew the soul out of the wood and vanished. The wooden stick in my left hand became a sword while the other one a torch. I immediately killed the disguised human body in the Devol. I sent its soul through my tunnel of re-incarnation. I drew the Devol's black soul out and spit it into the fire. The other Devol tried to escape but met the same fate as his brother-in-arms.

I asked Mohabat if she knew a sacred place where we could hide the statue. It looked like the real Phra Si Sakyamuni, a gold-covered Buddha sitting on a cushion like the real Bangkok's Wat Suthat. The Devols were unable to steal the real statue. They almost managed to steal its soul. We began to suspect that the statue's soul might be a key to Devol's future victory at Jewl.

Both Mohabat and I noticed the statue resembled our friend, Buddha. Could it be possible that the Devols knew of Buddha's existence? Had they begun to make plans for his immortal soul? We had to hide Wat Suthat's soul to protect Buddha and Bangkok's most valuable statue. For now, the statue had to be without its soul.

Mohabat suggested a place in Mohaba. Although I knew this place, having seen her sneaking in there, I pretended I did not know. I asked her for directions. After deciding where to place Wat Suthat's soul, I procured an animal's soul from one of the dragon statues in Bangkok's Temple. I asked the dragon if it would be willing to help us carry the heavy Phra Si Sakyamuni's soul to Mohabat's cave far from Bangkok. After we explained what seemed at stake, the dragon agreed. We deposited the statue in Mohabat's cave. I dispatched its soul into my violin tunnel so it could not recollect Mohabat's sacred cave. The dragon returned peacefully to its home. I made sure that the dragon's next life would be of another dragon statue back in the Temples.

5

MOHABAT'S SACRED PLACE OF TREASURE

After an exhausting night in Bangkok, Mohabat and I rested in her beautiful sacred cave which she found long ago. It was where she kept many unique treasures she collected over the centuries. It was up to me to release the souls of her collection if necessary. We inspected all her treasures. I was concerned some of them belonged to the Devols. I warned Mohabat to let go of some of them if not all. But she was unwilling to hear me out. She believed if they raised emotions in her that they must belong to her teenage years. They would help bring her memory back.

I doubted whether Mohabat's treasures were safe. I warned her, "It would be unwise for you to hold onto these things."

"I do not see anything wrong with them. I found them abandoned in the woods."

"It does not matter. You cannot keep them unless you are certain they are not possessed." One item troubled me, a wooden face mask. It belonged to the natives. I explained to Mohabat, "That facemask is used by the natives for their dance ceremonies." I warned her, "I am afraid that most of these items in your collection are haunted."

"How so?"

"They have owners. They belong to other spiritual beings." I picked up the mask, not seconds passed, I heard a group of spirits approaching the cave. My presence had woken the mask's spirit. It had called out to its native friends.

I grabbed Mohabat's hand and we left the cave to confront the spirits.

Mohabat feared, "Mahboo, I am scared. What do we do? What do we do?"

I looked at Mohabat but did not say a word. I held the mask in my left hand, ready to surrender.

Soon, a group of native souls surrounded us, wearing wooden masks. They flew in the air with their face-painted masks. They formed a fire outside. They circled side by side, flying around the fire. The head of the spirits, conspicuous by his hat that was adorned with feathers, flew cautiously down to our level. He approached us closely enough that we could see his wrinkles which distinguished his face.

He asked Mohabat and me, "Have you ever seen us, the spiritual natives, before?"

"No," I lied. The headman detected my fear. He walked closer to read both Mohabat's and my soul. He speedily grasped that the both of us were foreign spirits with substantial powers. He stepped backward, observing his circle of forest masks.

"I am the spiritual leader of Mohaba's natives," he announced.

I interrupted. "We understand. How can we help you?"

"I am here because you are keeping one of our valuable totems. Your cave has evil spirits preventing me from taking what is rightfully ours." He spoke slowly. We recognized his authority.

I hesitated. I wanted to protect Mohabat. Many spirits could have been disguised as anything, from an eagle to a fish to a bear to the moon or scarier, the sun itself. The natives had powerful spiritual capabilities. I tried to compose myself. I promised the leader I had not stolen their valuables intentionally. Mohabat wanted to say something but I hinted at her to stay silent by exchanging glances. She understood.

We promised the leader we would go back inside and bring anything that belonged to them. Mohabat and I went back inside to find the totems. Once inside, I whispered to Mohabat, "This happened, you know, because of me. I wake souls. I bring out souls in things. These natives located us because of that." While we collected all the totems that we could find, I told Mohabat, "I usually try to stay away from the native's belongings and their artwork. I respect them. To be honest, I am also scared of them." We left the cave with arms full of native artifacts. We returned them to their leader, the group began dancing around the fire to celebrate the return of their lost spiritual friends. As they danced, the spirits of the totems and statues wafted from the wood and joined the celebration.

Mohabat and I got invited to join them. We hesitated, remembering our responsibility to save Mohaba. It seemed disrespectful not to join. We began to dance. Happiness seeped into my soul. I had not been this happy since the day Mohabat passed away. I celebrated our reunion. Mohabat acted cheerfully.

The spirits appeared curious about us. The strong connection between the natives and us generated enough power to fuel the fire that lit up the whole forest area. Once the dance ended, the leader of the tribe thanked Mohabat and me for returning their lost spirits. He held both our hands and stared into our eyes, seeming to make eye contact with our souls. He asked us to call him by his real name, "Alo Hopi", which, he explained, means spiritual guide.

While Alo gazed into our eyes, I could see his genuine offer of friendship. I could feel his soul and read his thoughts. He said, "Together, we shall accomplish great things for Mohaba." Alo promised he would always be our confidante. "If you ever need guidance, whisper my name in your thoughts. I promise you will be heard. I promise my presence will appear where you are."

It seemed strange. Neither Mohabat nor I had said a word to Alo, yet he appeared to know who we were. He somehow knew our plans and what we were about to do for Mohaba.

He may have observed us in the forests. Once the dance ended, all the masked souls except Alo flew away. They blended into the moon.

Alo did not take his eyes off us. He repeated to us, "We shall be in touch soon. Do not forget. We will be in touch. Remember ..." His voice echoed as he faded away. The moon reflected off the ocean. All the creatures of Mohaba's forest were asleep. The rest seemed content with our encounter with their forest's strongest spiritual leader.

Mohabat and I went to the top of a nearby mountain to reflect on what had happened. It felt like one of Mohaba's peaceful nights. We had not enjoyed such peace in a long time. We were constantly engaged with interruptions. Before we knew it, the night had almost ended. We could see the endless reflection of the moon over the ocean.

Mohabat began talking to me, "How are we going to destroy all those treasures?"

"We will figure out a way."

"We were lucky tonight. But, what if ..." Mohabat worried the beasts would hurt us. My presence had woken some of them.

"For the time being, we are safe. The souls in these treasures cannot escape unless I am close." I pondered if we would ever be sitting in our heavenly garden enjoying each other's presence.

We stopped worrying about what unraveled around us. Everything started to feel at peace after our busy night in Bangkok and our encounter with the tribal guests. Mohabat, overwhelmed, "What an exhausting day, we made new forest friends and who can forget Bangkok."

I tried to comfort Mohabat, focusing on the bright side. "We survived it. That is what matters. We saved Buddha's statue's soul. We may have stopped his spirit from being shattered. We met a new team of spirits who we can count as our friends. They can help us protect the forests. They might even join us in the battle."

"You are right. I am more worried about the future than staying in this present, conscious of what we have accomplished tonight. It could not have happened without all your help. Thank you."

"Oh, Mohabat, you do not need to thank me. It is my obligation just as much as yours to protect our town. We are moving towards a goal, a good one."

Mohabat gained optimism. "That is true. I feel after such a long and I mean a long time, there seems to be hope, at last, now."

I held back my emotions. I comforted Mohabat while I felt my own soul to be comforted. I did not wish this moment to end.

Mohabat uttered in a calming voice as if she had forgotten the shocking news she had received in Bangkok, "I felt I am in a dream watching Alo Hop. Oh, sorry … I mean Alo Hopiiii. His tribe showing us their beautiful ceremony. I am extremely honored they welcomed us with open arms."

I agreed, "Of course, it is always nice to have new friends who can be there in time of need."

"If we ever must battle, we can count on our native friends to help us." Mohabat's heart seemed to warm up slightly.

"Yes, it is great."

"I had heard about them but never seen their spirits." Mohabat's heart remained warm. It became obvious to me that she felt at peace because we gained new allies in the forests.

"I never play with their spirits. They are awarded spirits of angels. It is their devotion to their lands. I try to stay out of their way. They like to keep to themselves, you know."

"It makes sense. I am glad they have sided with us, though." I read Mohabat's heart beating faster. It seemed as if a huge weight of responsibility has been lifted away from her. She could count on the native souls to guard the forests. I could read her mind while she imagined how nice it would be, for once, to leave the forest if she wished. The natives would guard it.

"I am, I am too." I stared out at the ocean. Mohabat moved her gaze towards the moon. The spirit Mohabat had never seen the moon this clearly before. The dark clouds were clearly present. They were blocking the moon. Even so, they had become invisible to me and Mohabat with our soul at peace. I may have unconsciously spread my invisible energy out to the sky, moon and ocean. It might have been the work of Alo Hopi. It did not matter to me, whom and how. It was a moment to cherish before a tough journey ahead of us.

"I did not know I was not allowed to have their totems. I had come to believe they were abandoned. Or else ..."

"That is all right, Mohabat." I was at peace. For once, I did not feel forced to pretend to be calm for Mohabat's sake. I was truly calm.

"I am glad they did not think we stole it from them or tonight would have turned out ugly."

"Of course not. He would not offer his friendship if he thought that we stole from them. He seemed grateful that we led them to it. We have nothing to worry about but should be grateful to gain new friends who now guard Mohaba's forests for us."

"True." Mohabat stopped, then expressed stubbornly, "We never finished our talk on how I was born. Do you feel up to telling me?"

"Umm, it is almost daylight but all right for you, of course." I did not want to leave Mohabat with the beautiful ocean visible to both of us and peaceful.

"Great."

"How about we go and sit by the fire the natives left behind? It is nice and warm, not that it makes us feel any warmer," I spoke in a funny voice with Mohabat giggling. For a moment, we both forgot what had happened to the world around us. Time stood still. It had not been like this for a long time.

"Oh, I thought you said I had a heart. If that is true then my heart is going to feel the warmth, is it not?" She whispered. "But … are you sure no one will hear us there?" She worried about waking more souls.

"I do not think you have anything to worry about." Neither

of us wanted another disaster. We had waited long enough for this day.

"Are you sure? I mean look at the native spirits …"

I interrupted, shocked, "What? Didn't you see in the cave? I heard them coming, didn't I?"

"That is true. I am sorry Mahboo, this night has been exhausting. We are lucky nothing bad happened to us."

"We are." I felt the need to explain, "You know I can hear the approach of any creature or spirit's soul. I will know if they are near or hear our conversation. You are safe with me." I comforted her. At the same time, I knew nothing is entirely certain in Mohaba. Even I, Death, can make grievous errors.

Mohabat appeared convinced. "I believe you."

"Well then, you know how you keep telling me you look up to me because you see that I am close to the universal gods."

"I do." Mohabat looked at me curiously.

"You also find me interesting because you believe some universal intelligence or maybe a higher being than me created me. Well, the truth is that, like me, you do not have any biological parents." I did not anticipate how Mohabat would respond. I expected a shocked reaction.

Mohabat, more curious than shocked asked, "What, no? Are you serious, no?"

"I am."

Mohabat, her curiosity turning to shock, probed, "How can that be possible? I died human." She always imagined her past as a human. She wore the outfit appropriate for a

17-year-old woman from centuries ago, the same one she died in.

"I guess you can call me your father. Weird, huh?"

"My father? You?" Mohabat's throat tightened. She was filled with confusion.

I paused for a moment before speaking, carefully planning my words. I answered her, "I could not believe it myself. It did happen. I hope this brings you closer to the truth."

"I am far from the truth, don't you think? Please tell me how it all happened?"

"Hmmm, when I first saw you, a naked baby, crawling in the rain and crying for help, I was amazed to be called in. I looked closely at your beautiful baby face. I saw your big brown eyes." I stopped to collect my thoughts. I had to make sure that I did not give away anything. After a short pause, I explained, "I could feel your whole soul shining. I knew some higher power had sent you with a mission. I did not know who had sent you, whether a universal intelligence or the gods. And, if so, why a human baby. But I knew you were special in some way."

"Oh. How about my immortality?"

"Right, you came with an immortal soul that belonged to you upon death. That is why you are a spirit and not re-birthed into new form."

"I see. Why do you think a baby?"

"I think they wanted a woman to be raised to become important. In your days, the majority were men with powers. I mean look at me, Death. I am male."

"Were there any clues left with me?"

I felt interrogated. "No."

"Well then, how do you know the invisible gods sent me? What if I was an abandoned baby?"

"I would have known if you had any biological parents. Trust me, I would have known."

"If you can feel people's souls, you probably can tell a lot from reading their minds. Would that be why you would know?"

I acted surprised. "How did you know I could do that?"

"You know there are books written about you. I can guess you read minds. You probably can read someone's entire life if you wanted."

"It is true. But … you must trust me, Mohabat. If you had parents, I would have returned you to them." I attempted to leave no doubts in Mohabat's mind after our conversation ended.

"No, I am curious. Of course, I trust you would have."

"Mohabat, you need to know that since you came to this world, I have changed my views about women. I know you are part of the universal gods' plan, placed here as a miracle." I urged to explain to her so her awkward past would make more sense somehow, although, I, myself, did not have any real answers for her.

"Right, I am not sure if I feel that way. Please do continue."

"I raised you to protect you. You were like me in some ways with some higher powers controlling your destiny. You are gifted with great powers." I focused on what was known. I tried to make it look clear. But, her uncertain entry to this world and her unique abilities seemed unclear to neither Buddha nor me. We did not know their purpose. I began to find it more difficult to convince her.

"I see."

"Good." I reacted assertively. I did not know what her future entailed. "I know this is hard. You will eventually see why. There is no other like you out there."

Mohabat, not knowing much about her past, asked, "Why can't you tell me everything?"

"It is for your own good. Your heart is not strong enough. It needs more time." I wanted to tell Mohabat everything. But, Buddha's advice kept me from losing control of our conversation.

"I can handle it. Haven't I handled my own team well?" Mohabat pulled back a little. She sounded mad and impatient.

I responded calmly, "It does not matter. You must trust me. Your heart is not ready to hear everything about your past. It is complicated."

"How complicated can it be?"

"Well, Buddha believes it is for the best that I tell you gradually in bits and pieces. But, do not worry, by the time we reach the end of it, you will understand more."

"How can I be sure of that?" Mohabat asked, feeling agitated. While remaining seated, she leaned back. I moved back to reach closer to her. She gazed at the moon while I quickly leaned back more. She turned her face to me.

I looked directly into her eyes and promised, "You have my word."

"I do not understand. I did not expect to hear that you are my father tonight."

I knew where Mohabat was going. I knew she was trying to get more information out of me. "Mohabat, listen to me. Right now, it is about the people, animals, and spirits of Mohaba who need your strength to save them."

"True, I know. I know. I do." Mohabat appeared let down.

"We need you to stay strong. Please be patient, just a little more."

"I guess I cannot question what happened. If you think it is not in my best interest then I will wait, for now." Mohabat appeared calmer but upset. She never liked waiting for things to unravel without her control.

"I am glad you have been this understanding about all of this." I wanted to encourage her to think about something else. "To be honest, I did not think you would be this understanding." I tried to soothe her impatience.

"I guess it is a good motivation for me. To work harder to get my internal strength ... to have my heart beat. But it seems odd. I never thought I had one."

"You do. You needed someone to help you realize it is there my ... friend." I almost called Mohabat "my love." I noticed that I was losing focus. At this point, I had to avoid discussing the past. We had to focus on saving Mohaba. For us, to get to that day of paradise, we had to put ourselves and our love last. I had no plans to let any distraction destroy our future happiness.

"I am not quite sure exactly why I am here to fight the Devols. Maybe it is written in my destiny. With that said, I think I can wait a little longer. But, I have waited centuries … but all right, I guess, a few more days will not hurt." My girl wanted badly to know. I could sense it in her. I decided to let go and focus on what was at stake.

"It is best for you to have your heart develop. This way, you are less likely to be ruined by the Devols."

"True."

"I have doubts about what their powers include. I mean … look at all the mystery surrounding Jewl. Who knows what they can do with it?"

"I do not know either. I mean, why did they steal Wat Suthat?"

"Exactly. I am quite concerned because it looks exactly like Buddha."

"It is possible they have plans to destroy him, or worse, take away his immortal gifts."

I continued, "That is why I think it is important for us to stay focused. We cannot afford to be defeated. We are responsible for the whole world, not just our town. Do you understand the risks, Mohabat?"

"Sure, I mean … I feel I am somewhat in the dark."

"You are but you do trust me, don't you?" I asked Mohabat feeling once again like her father.

"I have to trust the people I know care about me ... who want what is best for Mohaba and me," she forcefully uttered in frustration. Her heart slowed again. I spotted no warmth but coldness.

Mohabat hated being kept in the dark. As a leader, she has always been aware of everything around her. I placed her into the unknown for decades. I hoped to bring the conversation back to her heart. "We have enough time to build your heart. You should not worry. We cannot afford to lose you in battle. I will not let you go if you are not there yet."

"What happens if my heart is not developed? I want to know. What if, Mahboo, it does not beat by the time we go into battle?" Mohabat looked puzzled and lost.

"I pray that it does. I will not let you go with a fragile heart unless Master will not let me. If it does not, hmmm, I guess, it is easier to destroy you. There is no heart to keep your immortal soul alive."

"I am until this present time immortal, aren't I? Why the need for my heart to work?"

"Your immortal soul can easily be taken away or stolen from you. It has no associated heart owning it."

"Oh OK, well then ..."

I meddled, "You need your eternal heart beating because you have powerful fighting skills necessary to destroy these monsters. We cannot afford to lose you to them."

"Well, I hope I can get my heart beating then but, um, you cannot blame me for worrying."

"I do not."

"There have been so many weird things happening. I am starting to worry."

"Well, it is hard to predict right now what will happen before we head to Jewl."

"I am tired of seeing our people tortured. I want it to stop."

"I do too. We have a good chance of defeating them. Look at tonight. We were surrounded by lots of danger. We survived it."

"True, we did but I am concerned."

"I understand you are. It is natural."

"Mohaba's ghosts are hungry for vengeance. They are all waiting for justice. I fear them hating me."

"Why would you think that?" I could not believe Mohabat's negative thoughts.

Mohabat went on, "They probably hate me. I am or at least, I think I am the most skilled fighter."

"Why would they hate you? They should praise you and be happy they have someone who can protect them in the forests."

"No, you do not understand. They should hate me. I have not done anything to fight back these Devols, never."

"Do not say that Mohabat."

"I mean, all these years, I did not try on my own to see if I could, you know. I am weak."

"You are entertaining weak thoughts. Listen to me. You are wise waiting for the right time."

"You are saying this to make me feel better."

"No, you are getting more skilled with practice. If this

town is going to get rid of the Devols, they cannot expect to do it through one being against all those evils."

"I know. I know, we have to work together." Mohabat leaned away from me.

"It cannot be done with one. I did not proceed either, Mohabat. Please do not feel bad."

Mohabat turned to face me. "True," she replied with optimism returning to her voice.

"Just because you are chosen does not mean you are supposed to do this all by yourself. You know that, don't you?"

"In some ways, yes, I do."

"We are saving all of Mohaba. All the creatures of Mohaba have to come together to help or there is no purpose to the fight, is there?"

"I know Mahboo … it should be all of us together. We will be more powerful and less likely defeated."

"Exactly, glad you agree now." I finally became pleased.

"I am tired of watching the things they are doing to us. I want the torture to end."

"That is why we cannot do this alone. We can do it now because Jewl is available to us."

"We do have to act fast. It does not make sense for Mohaba this close to the gods to be in this much misery, Mahboo. Enough is enough. We … all of us in Mohaba deserve to be happy."

"Yes, we sure deserve it."

"It is possible the higher beings warned us; maybe the thunder and Jewl's reappearing was not an accident."

I agreed with her although Buddha had expressed doubt about this. I smiled, "I think so too."

"I am glad we finally agree on something." Mohabat giggled. To make her point, she touched my left shoulder with her right hand. She did it to make a point. I felt a moment's hesitation before she took away her hand.

I felt Mohabat and I bonded with her not as human but as a spirit. "You know I am Death, viewed by many spirits as a beast. I am hated by many and believed to be a Devol."

"First, that is because they do not know you. Secondly, they are not smart enough to realize that you take a life at the gods' request. Thirdly, you are making the circle of life exist." Mohabat's innocent touch on my shoulder seemed to have strengthened our bond.

"I know but …"

Mohabat intervened, "If it were not for you, they would not exist. I would not exist. You are the reason we are here. They are fools."

"Thanks, Mohabat. You are sweet, you know that? There is a reason I named you Mohabat, you know."

"Really? What does it mean?"

"It is an old ancient word for kindness."

Mohabat shockingly asked, "Kindness?"

"Yes, it is because you are kind. You have been this way since you were born. Now, with your warriors."

"I try my best. Oh, Mahboo, you are right. We need to deal with the tough journey ahead of us first. I am confident; we will have plenty of time to go over my past. It is sad to see Devols manage Mohaba for such a long time."

I found we were back to the same old conversation. I clarified, "It is what it is. We have to deal with what is important now."

"We will defeat these vicious invaders." Mohabat sounded hopeful once again. She used the same tone of voice she always used as a leader to get her team excited.

I resisted the temptation to tell Mohabat everything. "I know you are confused about your past. We needed to protect you after your death, Mohabat, by never letting you know who you are, by leaving no memory of your human life."

Mohabat puzzled, "By 'we,' do you mean you and the Buddha?"

I clarified, "No, Buddha was not around then. I mean the gods of the universe, the higher powers and me. We had to ensure your safety. Look at the Devols. If you had your memory, they would have read your mind by now and, who knows, maybe you would not be here."

"I see." Mohabat sounded confused. She said what she thought was appropriate.

"It was for your own protection," I tried to convince Mohabat.

"With good intentions, I have no doubt we will. I do not doubt you Mahboo, not anymore. I have no reason not to trust you anymore. You are spending your time with me, even now, it means a lot."

"Higher powers had and have big plans for you. You are

destined to do great things for Mohaba. I have no doubt." I tried to sound enthusiastic.

"I am starting to understand why I am different from all the other Angelious."

"You are."

"Aha, before, I felt kind of out-of-place, cursed, over these centuries."

I was shocked to hear Mohabat felt negative about her situation. "Why would you feel this way?"

"Well, you are doing what the gods have planned for you but what about me? Nothing is clear to me."

"No, you cannot think this way. You need to stop these thoughts now. You are blessed. You are forgetting how you have been a great leader to your team. You taught them how to battle, kept them entertained."

"I know Mahboo. That is because I had to do something to pass the time. We built a team but were not strong to face the Devols."

I had reached my limit. "I will not listen to this anymore."

"I do not know if you are right."

"You have managed to stay here. That on its own is worth something. You will live up to your destiny one day, I promise you that."

"I do not see how different I am from other spirits. I have no doubt that you have your reasons and some backup too perhaps."

"Mohabat, you cannot see your own soul like I do."

"True. I do not."

"You have no idea how many spirit souls would want to change places with you. You own an immortal soul. Only a few in the world have this gift. You and Buddha are amongst them."

"I have no choice but to believe you," Mohabat stressed, "At least, until I find out exactly what happened in my past."

I tried to approach her concerns from a different direction. "Mohabat, have you ever been with your friends somewhere and seen something that distracted you?"

"Yes, many times."

"You are in a place that you enjoy but become distracted by an insect buzzing around the room. You wish that you could kill it. It would stop distracting you."

"I have. How do you know I am often distracted?"

"I am Death. I see things others do not pay attention to. Do you want me to finish the story?"

"Yes, I do. What happens? Tell me."

"An insect like a flying beetle interrupts your conversation. You do not react immediately. You just watch and wait."

"Sure, and ..." Mohabat turned her gaze to the night sky where the dark clouds slowly reappeared. Only the ocean was visible. The sun rises. The clouds began to block our view. As we watched, the ocean turned from navy to black and to blue. We could smell the salty air that rose from the sands on the beach. But it did not stop us from continuing our conversation.

I noticed the change in the weather but continued, "Well, you do not distract the rest of your team by going after the beetle. You continue as if everything is moving on normally. When the time is right, say the beetle has landed somewhere, you throw a rock at it and destroy it."

"It is true. I have done this many times. I do not try to kill it when it is flying."

"Exactly."

Mohabat annoyed asks, "What is your point?"

"My point is that right now, we know how to destroy the Devols. We have found them in one spot just like the annoying beetle. There is a place that is key to eliminating them. We have been waiting for this moment for the insect to land so we can destroy it."

"Still, what does that have to do with finding out about my past?" Stubborn Mohabat, distracted by the smell of the ocean went back to asking about her past.

I tried to get Mohabat to notice how her continuous interest in her past is distracting her from what is important. I concluded, "Your past is the conversation you are trying to have with your friends but you have found the beetle and you want to destroy it."

"Alright Mahboo, I understand what you are saying. I will not ask you again. We focus on killing the beetle. In the end, I am going to find out. I trust you will not leave me after, will you?"

"Why would you think I would leave you?"

"Well, you never met me until now. Where were you before?"

"Before, I was busy trying to save the world … control all the troubles Devols were causing here."

"I see, but you are promising me, Mahboo, you will not leave me after the battle. You will tell me everything." She gazed deeply into my eyes waiting for reassurance.

I finished our talk. "I promise." Mohaba went back to appearing dead and dark.

6

THE CROW TOTEM AND THE WARRIORS

A night of chaos and discoveries and an alliance with powerful natives unraveled hastily in the woods. The rising sun was no more than a shadow of the dark clouds when Mohabat headed home. The voices of crows cawed over her head. She was never fond of crows, or black cats. Their blackness reminded her of the Devols who possessed creatures at dark nights to capture prey. The increasing presence of crows around Jewl made Mohabat wonder if the Devols possessed the crows like they did with the hyenas. If so, they were less identifiable than previous incarnations.

Mohabat attempted to move her gaze towards one of the crows' eyes. She found them impossible to read. Another crow became particularly loud, its voice probing deep into Mohabat's brain.

Mohabat planned to isolate herself to revisit the moments from the night before. She strode towards her cave, the crow's piercing cries increased her agitation. She wanted to run inside but paused and turned to gaze back at the burnt woods. Dark energy was present with the remains of the woods from the fire dance. It could only mean more chaos ahead.

Mohabat turned once again to run inside, she stepped on something hard. She instantly adopted a warrior stance and approached it. It was no more than a block of wood, she relaxed. Mohabat leaned over and picked it up. It was a carved crow, a totem of some kind. She became bothered worrying how it ended up by her step. She guessed that a Devol crow discovered her lair.

Mohabat feared immensely falling victim to the Devols. She recalled Phra Si Sakyamuni statue. Both Mohabat and I suspected from Bangkok that Buddha was close to becoming a victim of the Devol's master deception. It appeared to us that they wanted to replace Buddha's soul with Wat Suthat's statue. Now, anxious, Mohabat expected that it might be her turn.

Mohabat forgot for a moment about her past, which she suspected ended tragically. She held the wooden crow with both hands. It was about the size of her torso. She examined the totem and a breeze emanated. She looked up. She saw Alo Hopi approaching.

Alo spoke calmly, "Mohabat, I cannot tell you who stole our totem and placed it here."

Mohabat handed the totem to Alo. "I want you to know that I did not steal it."

"Oh please, Mohabat. I know you did not."

"I am afraid Devols have found out about us all."

"No, no." Alo took the totem in his left hand. He twisted his arm to conceal the totem behind him. "I promise you that the soul inside this totem belongs to my own team. It is safe. It is not possessed."

"Are you positive?"

"Yes, I am."

"Then who would do such a thing?"

"That I am not quite sure of."

Mohabat, looking worried asked Alo, "What do you think it means?"

"It must be another kind of creature." Alo continued to hide the totem.

"Great. We are not safe from the Devols. Now, we have to fear another evil force."

Alo's voice firm, "We will find out who did this." Keeping the totem hidden behind his back, Alo released its spirit. It flew away into the forest. "Mohabat, I promise. Do not let this distract you, my dear." He departed.

Mohabat turned to take a last look at the clearing, reliving her dance with Mahboo. She returned to her team of warriors. They openly welcomed her but with suspicion. Mohabat never abandoned them more than half a day. They shouted,

"Where have you been? We have been practicing non-stop without you."

She smiled. "Well, to tell you the truth, I spent my entire evening until early morning with a gentleman." Then, admonishing them, she said, "But, I never instructed you to practice all night and day, did I?"

The shocked warriors ignored Mohabat's last comment. "A gentleman?" They said in unison, looking at her and then at each other, suspicion written on their faces. Turning back to Mohabat, they waited for her to reveal more.

All the warriors witnessed Mohabat's failed attempts at finding love. They were skeptical. "But Mohabat, how did you find this man worthy of you?" She refused to give them details thereby increasing the implausibility of such an event in their minds.

While chattering about Mohabat's news, the warriors spotted an enormous crow approaching, its wingspan large enough to encompass the entire group. Even though no creature other than Buddha and I had seen the Angelious before, the crow recognized Mohabat. Everyone disturbed by the crow's ability to identify their leader suspected the gentleman, me, of betraying Mohabat.

An Angelious shouted, "The dark side, perhaps the Devols, have discovered us. Act fast, we got to kill it now." Their voice echoed.

The crow attempted to pluck Mohabat with its long beak. I noticed the odd distrustful activity. I showed up invisible. I hit the crow as hard as I could. It fell to the ground, stunned, but soon bounced back. It detected my presence and frantically flapped its wings to escape. But it was too late. I took its soul. To my surprise, it did not disappear. Instead, it transformed into a wild dog and quickly vanished into the woods. Luckily, the Angelious had not seen me. They breathed sighs of relief. Nevertheless, they were afraid their identities had now been revealed to the dark forces. Almost all of them suspected that the man Mohabat spent her evening with was somehow responsible.

Mohabat left the group hastily without saying a word. The Angelious followed her and stopped her. "We need to know what just happened there. Where are you going? Have you forgotten about your team?"

Mohabat did not share much with her group except promising that she would return with some answers. Mohabat's immortal soul healed her from a bruise caused by the crow's attempt to pick her up. She had no idea what had happened. The crow totem came to her mind. Mohabat guessed there was a connection between the two events. Now, she knew she had fallen victim to something beyond her control. I worried Mohabat might have been injured. I found her in the woods where she was looking for me.

I had no idea of the crow's identity. "We are not safe," we both said.

"What was that, Mahboo?"

"I am not quite sure." We did not feel the creature possessed a Devol spirit. Devols never transform into another creature.

"It must be the same being who placed the totem by my entrance."

For once, I felt I was in the dark unaware of Mohaba's unfolding events. "What totem?"

"Oh, sorry Mahboo, I did not have a chance to tell you."

"Tell me what?"

"After our talk, I headed back to my cave. Right by my entrance, someone, or something, had placed a large wooden crow right by my doorstep. Even Alo did not know what or whom," Mohabat shook her head.

"Why did you not call out for me? I might have been able to help spot the creature."

"Sorry, I did not know how to call for you. You never taught me how"

"Oh," I brought both my hands to my face. I sighed as I moved them back down to my side. "How could I have forgotten too? I assumed, I guessed, you would know how." I felt horrible.

"Well, tell me now then."

"Right. If you call out for me in your thoughts, I will hear your voice. I will come to you. Sorry, I should have told you this earlier."

"That is all right. So, what do you think this creature or being or whatever it is, is trying to communicate? Please tell me it is not the Devols. Or, we are doomed. Alo says it is not."

"Well, what happened to the totem?"

"I think Alo set its spirit free. Or, at least, I believe he did."

"I see. If Alo could not read anything into it, then I would not have been able to either. No point searching for it now." Both Mohabat and I remained silent for a few minutes.

"What do we do now?" Mohabat asked.

"For the Angelious' safety, I advise you, Mohabat, to be as cautious as you can be."

"Yes, of course. Always." Mohabat nodded.

I cautioned her, "Try to pay more attention to your surroundings."

"I can try to do my best, but, do you think it is safe for me to stay in the woods while this creature is possibly planning to take my soul away from me?"

"Hmmm," my voice echoed. I took a moment to think. Mohabat surprisingly stayed silent. I could sense she was nervous. She is normally talkative. She only became silent when she was anxious. I could see the pain and worry in her eyes. I remembered Buddha's advice to not upset Mohabat. We needed Mohabat's strength. I did not think it would be wise to have her stay in the forests.

Mohabat had not moved and forced her word. "Well …"

"We will avoid the forests. We will arrange to meet inside your cave. Make sure it is shielded by the angelic spirits so it is the safest place possible for us to meet."

"It seems like a good plan, plausible. Thank you, but wait, I do need to talk to my team. Let them know I will not be around for a while."

"Yes, of course."

Mohabat relaxed now that we had a plan.

I said, "I suspect this creature is working for the Devols."

Mohabat, shocked, "Really? Why is that?"

I stared into Mohabat's eyes. I made sure she was calm before I continued. "Remember how Devols were trying to steal Buddha's statue's soul. Maybe they want to steal yours."

"I know. That is what I suspected at first. But, Alo does not believe it is true."

"Maybe Alo is right but we need to be prepared for the worst possible case."

Mohabat agreed, "Exactly."

"I think they or it … may have overheard our plans. If so, our entire existence may be in jeopardy. If that is, the creature is connected to the Devols."

"It could. Who knows? All these weird things have been happening since we went to Bangkok."

"I know. That is because we are on the right track. Trust me."

Mohabat moved closer. "That is good to hear."

"Yes, we need to make sure we do not fall into their trap. The crow or whatever this creature is, easily transformed into a wild dog. I did not sense a Devol. If it is working for them, it might be trying to stop us from getting to Jewl. Who knows what they are guarding."

Mohabat sighed, "I know. I better go and talk to my team."

I left Mohabat comfortable in the knowledge that she could call out for my help at any time. We were all busy. I had my normal duties in addition to planning a way to find out what was inside Jewl. We needed to discover what other powerful enemies we might be battling. Mohabat returned to her friends to warn them about a new threat to the forests.

Mohabat assured her Angelious group that they had nothing to worry about. She suspected that the creature wanted her soul and not theirs. She told them she had to stay away from the forests for some time. She comforted them by assigning an invisible angel to watch out for their welfare. Mohabat realized how dangerous it would be to talk openly anymore. Now her concerns about her past life did not seem so important.

To comfort Mohabat and make her feel safe again, I cleared out only the strange items from her collection. Mohabat had created the cave as a refuge that the Devols could not access. The wooden crow was left at Mohabat's door suggesting that the unknown being could not access her cave. The native spirits could not sense their lost totems until I stepped inside and woke them up. It seemed to be the safest place for Mohabat to stay until we figured out what to do next.

Meanwhile, the Devols were bonding. We hoped that we had found our beetle's vulnerable spot—Jewl. We did not yet know what kind of rock to throw. So far, we were mostly reacting to problems as they raised their heads. We seemed to have a direction and a plan and yet were struggling to protect our identities. It could be the bad energy in the air created by the Devols. I did not see meeting Alo as a bad thing. We needed more allies. Mohabat did not know that the bad energy could partly be a result of my being in the world, a world that is dangerous and attracts death.

The Angelious warriors started searching for the spirit that sent out the bad energy to their forest. This unknown threat made their preparations for the battle more difficult. Despite the challenges, the Angelious were confident in their martial skills. They knew they were good enough for the battle ahead. They were well trained. The group had originally been made up of women, but over time, equally spiritual men who possessed similar skills joined the team. Most of them had become lovers who sometimes, practiced passionately late at night. They were determined to put their skills to the test searching for Mohaba's mysterious spirit.

7

THE TWIN SISTERS OF MOHABA

Mohabat was one of the few creatures who had access to Jewl. We discovered this on the night she left her group. We hovered around Jewl, looking for clues.

As we flew around Jewl, Mohabat asked me in whispered voice, "Can you see that spot clear of Devols? Please place me there."

"On its rooftop? No, it is dangerous." I hoped to change Mohabat's mind. I flew the opposite direction.

"Mahboo, can you for once listen to me? Please go back."

"You are going to be visible. Unless, you want me to be seen by the Devols then ..."

"Of course not, I will call out to you if I feel unsafe. You do not have to lend me your gown."

"Alright but be super careful." I stopped insisting. I headed back to where Mohabat had asked me to drop her off. Luckily, there were no signs of Devols in that area.

I placed Mohabat down on Jewl's rooftop. To my amazement, she did not get noticed. She passed through the roof's protected shield as if she was a Devol herself. I could not quite figure out how. It probably had to do with her golden spirit. She passed through extremely guarded shields without attracting any of the Devol's attention.

I nattered in my thoughts, "You can access Jewl, what a relief."

"See, I told you I could." Mohabat glimpsed from the top. In her thoughts, she chatted, "I see an empty room with lots of hanging items on the wall."

"There are plenty of rooms. Our luck, there seems to be nothing in this one."

"I want to check out the other ones." Mohabat curiously moved towards the right end of the roof with no Devols nearby. She headed to view another room with her head passed the woods. A Devol headed towards where Mohabat was. I warned her, "Stop, there is a Devol approaching." I moved close enough to grab Mohabat from her waist. She had her head inside the shields. I had to pull her out and fast.

Mohabat excited, "Well, that was close. At least, we know I can go inside. This is great news for Mohaba."

"Not quite."

"Why not?"

"You have to consider there may be creatures that might discover you in there."

"But this is the only way we can find out what the Devols are up to. We have no other way to access Jewl, you know that, right."

"That is true but there must be another way. We have not found it but we will. We need to search more." I placed Mohabat down on the ground. She moved away. I pulled aside allowing her to step out of my gown. By then, we had reached back to the forest. We were, again, far away from Jewl.

We brainstormed for hours while back at Mohabat's place. She kept on keenly insisting, "I can go inside and have you watch me. You warn me when Devols come around. I will follow your instructions; it is not that complicated, is it?"

"It is extremely risky. You can get discovered." I took a step closer to Mohabat. Our face almost touched. My parental concern took over. I was about to hold her but I controlled myself not to.

Mohabat reached for a nearby rock and sat down. "I know Mahboo. You saw nothing happened to me."

"Right. Do not forget who came to rescue you?"

"Alright, I know it is dangerous. I trust you will watch me carefully and if needed, save me again."

I sat beside Mohabat. I convinced her, "I cannot promise you, my dear. I may be called to show up elsewhere. I cannot risk sending you in there like that. But ..."

"But, what? Tell me."

I gazed at Mohabat. I strongly had doubts. We had done this in the past. We witnessed failure. Here we are, decades later, we are dealing with the consequences of our action. But, the thoughts of letting Devols rule Mohaba for another day forced me to go ahead and agree. "Alright, I can lend you my gown. You cannot be seen."

"No Mahboo, I cannot demand this of you. What if you get discovered? What if something bad happens to you?"

"I have gone without my gown before."

"Still ..."

"Mohabat, I know how to protect myself."

"I hope so. I am doubting now if we should go through with this."

"The worse, if I need my gown back, I will call out to you. You will come back out with it. Do not worry."

"Are you positive, Mahboo? I do not know; I do not know if it is such a good idea now."

"No, we both know it is time to stand up for our people. We will survive this and bring back victory to Mohaba." Mohabat and I realized the urgency to act quickly.

Mohabat was not safe in the woods. The timing was perfect. By sending her inside Jewl, we would find out if the Devols noticed an intruder. From behind a tall thick aged tree nearby, I carefully observed Mohabat's every move. My gown seemed to fit her well. Her slim body blended well into my gown. I used my tree shaped bowl filled with mirror water to watch her. I saw her approach Jewl. I whispered in my thought through my bowl. I could hear her thoughts returning to me, "Jewl does not look like an abandoned castle. I smell torture. I sense a lot of hidden treasures and souls."

I talked to Mohabat in my thought, "The rooms are filled with spirits. Do not worry, they do not appear threatening. You are safe to carry on." The more Mohabat walked passed each room, the more confident I became about the spirits not appearing dangerous nor belonging to the Devols. As Mohabat moved silently through the mansion, we noticed many unique caged creatures and animals. I thought back to when it used to be a lively home. Now, it had become an unbelievably dark place.

Mohabat said in her thoughts, "It smells like old wood here. So much dust, it is unbearable. I am glad that I am not human. I sense it but lucky I do not have to inhale any of this." I watched Jewl through Mohabat with my bowl. The only light came through the cracked wood covering the windows and holes in the roof. How had the Devols acquired the wood and put it up? Had they had human help? These questions niggled at me as Mohabat struggled to see through the dimmed surroundings.

Soon, Mohabat came upon a stunning sight. It had a fountain in a lake. I noticed sooner than her the many small sharks swimming around in circles. Mohabat, terrified, asked me, "Do you believe I am safe to be here?" I worried about her being thrown into the fountain and eaten by the sharks. There seemed to be something odd about the swimming sharks. They appeared to belong to a different world. I could not quite tell yet if Mohabat had the power to protect herself from these unknown creatures. I took the risk by telling her to carry on.

I began to regret sending her inside. I whispered encouragement to her, hiding my worry. For a moment, Mohabat seemed relieved behind her worried eyes. She then talked to me in her thoughts, "I am so grateful, Mahboo, for not being human right now or else ..." I stopped her. I tried to convince Mohabat that she is safe to go into the fountain area. For once, after hearing her say she is glad not be human, I did not feel guilty for taking her human life away from her.

Soon, I noticed spirits observing Mohabat's every move. I hoped that they were good. Mohabat came across some spirits in drawings on the wall. They had teeth like vampires. I wondered whether Kerman dreamt about becoming a vampire. The vibe and surroundings suggested that. Unless, he had been obsessed with vampires. We both had not seen unique sea animals swimming amongst the sharks before. I had not seen these creatures for many decades. They now looked different. I assumed they had been extinct.

Mohabat spotted a big seahorse with the same vampire teeth. These creatures were thought to be extinct. I became unsure as to what my eyes had seen. I wondered about the common factor — the vampire teeth. Could a vampire destroy a Devol? Was this the reason they were keeping them captive at Jewl?

I had been uncertain whether Devols had blood. Maybe the vampire-like teeth were designed for sucking out souls, not blood. I felt more confused than before Mohabat entered

Jewl. I felt like we reached a dead end. We had more questions than when we started.

Mohabat stared at the sea horses in the small fountain lake. She drew her attention to a unique huge fish that shined in gold. Like the sea horses, it swam unafraid among the sharks. I concluded that the Devols kept the sharks well fed. Not soon after, a mermaid emerged from the depths of the lake. She swam accosted among the sharks. I had told Mohabat stories of mermaids when she was a child. I never believed they existed. And yet, here it was, a mermaid swimming lazily among sharks. It swam slowly along the golden fish in this oddly tiny lake.

Many of the rooms Mohabat had passed through were adorned with mirrors containing living souls that watched with curiosity. I wondered if they could see her or sense her presence. I saw Pretas, ghosts, fly freely around the rooms. They are known to be hungry for revenge against Devols. It appeared that the Devols had cast a spell, locking them in Jewl. They seemed to be repeating certain words over and over. It seemed like they were trying to discover a secret word that would break Devols' spell.

I could tell the Pretas were hungry for revenge against the Devols. To my amusement, they did not notice spirit Mohabat. It helped that she had my gown on. Without it, I would guess she would have been discovered and who knows, maybe caged or destroyed.

I heard the Pretas repeat, "We hate Delorah. She is the ugliest woman inside and out. She must be destroyed with the rest of the Devols. We must find the magic word." I did not know a person named Delorah. The Pretas were clearly working to decode a spell or a sequence of words to set them free.

Most of the creatures in Jewl, like the Pretas, were ignored and abandoned. We discovered that not all the creatures were of the afterlife. The sharks were real and not spirits. We anticipated finding animal creatures and maybe captive humans. Mohabat watched the swimming animals, a woman emerged from behind the rocks near the lake and began to feed the sea creatures. While this young woman fed the animals, a mermaid came out of the water. It transformed into a full woman.

Awfully scared, Mohabat hid behind a rocky mound from where she could watch. She reassured me, "I got this. They do not know I am here." The mermaid's vampire teeth showed as it talked to the strange Devol woman who the Pretas despised. I suspected her to be who Pretas called Delorah. She had her back to the mermaid. Mohabat could only see the mermaid's face but could not hear well. The noise of the fountain and the water falling off the rocks interrupted.

I carried on observing everything through Mohabat's eyes and her surroundings. While holding my bowl, and watching, I spotted an eagle circling above me. Her reflection brought my attention to her. The eagle's reflection interfered with my view of Mohabat. I worried the eagle contained the spirit of the crow I had killed earlier. For a while, its presence did not concern me. I became confident it would not understand what I was doing. I decided to ignore it.

I soon found the eagle's presence distracting. I had to get rid of it. Mohabat seemed fine watching the two women talking. She barely could hear their conversation. If the eagle was not in my way, I would have tried to listen in. I called out to Mohabat, "Are you OK? You think you are safe for few minutes?" She answered, "I think so. I am not confident they can sense me Mahboo. They do not seem to know I am watching them. I guess I am all right, for now."

Confident Mohabat would be fine for the next few moments, I abandoned my wooden bowl. I flew up to reach the eagle. I got close, it transformed itself into one of Mohaba's thickest trees. It seemed to be a clever creature. It knew I would be reluctant to take the soul of an ancient tree. The ancient trees live a long life. They transform into a newly planted tree should a tragedy strike. And it takes a long time to take a tree's soul. So, the eagle knew I would hesitate. I was perplexed at how the strange creature knew my identity. I could only guess.

The eagle chose to transform itself into an ancient tree. It knew that I would struggle to take its soul. But it bothered me and distracting me from the job at hand. Somehow, I distinguished the eagle had a woman's soul. I guessed it to be the same creature that had appeared as a crow. It attempted to kidnap Mohabat earlier. Now, I knew it had to be a female of some sort. It had to be someone with great powers who could change forms. I needed to figure out how to destroy her.

But while I tried to take the ancient tree's soul, Mohabat had finally seen Devol Delorah's face. She shouted, drawing the attention of every being inside Jewl. As she recounted later, she tried to reach me. I did not respond. She thought she had lost contact with me. She had become extremely anxious with me being unreachable. Mohabat's scream scared the other women. The mermaid jumped back into the water and swam away. Delorah moved closer to Mohabat, who remained frozen. Delorah took one look at Mohabat and, much to her surprise, she began shouting at her.

Mohabat could not move. The other Devols, hearing the shouts, sent one of their soldiers down to check on Delorah. But Delorah had left Jewl as fast as she could. She thought she had lost her mind. I saw her leaving Jewl. I approached her. "Oh, thank God Mohabat. Are you all right? I am terribly sorry ... I looked away to take care of this extremely annoying eagle that spied on us." Mohabat looked puzzled. The confused woman asks me, "Who are you. My name is not Mohabat. It is Delorah. Wait a minute. I know you. You are Death. Do you remember me from a long time ago?"

I was shocked to find out I was not talking to Mohabat. Another woman, identical to Mohabat stood in front of me. Mohabat had been turned into a Devol. I felt sick with fear and guilt. I had been distracted from the task of watching over Mohabat. Now, the Devols had taken her.

If Delorah had not spoken up, I would have rushed into Jewl, risking my cover to look for the real Mohabat. But Delorah asked, "Does this all have anything to do with the woman I saw who looks like me?" She seemed as confused by what had happened. Could I trust her?

I went back to my wooden bowl full of water. I needed to figure out what happened to my girl. Delorah stood beside me. I did not feel comfortable with her standing near me. She knew a lot about my identity.

I grabbed my tree bowl. I saw to my great relief that Mohabat was alive inside Jewl. But I saw a couple of Devols looking for her. . I grabbed Delorah's hand tight with force and placed it into the water. The water turned cloudy. It turned black as if an ink was thrown in. I took her hand out of the bowl of water.

I looked at Delorah. She was a Devol. Perhaps she had the answer. I placed my hand on her forehead, as I do when I am about to take a life, to see if I could learn anything. By gods' decree, I am only to do this when about to take a life. We saw Delorah's life played out as if on a stage in a theater. Delorah had the ability to watch the play as I did—and like me, we were both shocked to discover the truth about her past. For what had unfolded in front of us appeared like the life story of another, of my beloved Mohabat. The play revealed to us the unspeakable truth. Delorah was Mohabat's identical twin sister.

Just as I had found Mohabat as a baby, Delorah had been found and raised by Devols. The Devols were amazed by Delorah's spiritual powers. They wanted her for her immortal gift. Delorah's destiny to grow up with her sister, Mohabat, had been altered by the Devols. They had stolen her life. They used her to help them do evil things. Delorah had no idea of her past. She had come to believe that the Devols were her family.

Sadness and outrage took over her. She reminded me of Mohabat when she appeared upset. It appeared to me that Delorah had not been inherently evil. Devols had raised her to carry out their evil tasks. I could read Delorah's extreme rage of feeling betrayed by her Devol family. Delorah did not seem as sad as some humans do when they find out their family had betrayed them. She became more relieved than angry to discover she had been their prisoner. It perhaps explained some of the discomforts she had always felt among her Devol family, a feeling that she had been an outsider.

But Delorah became a valuable discovery for me. She had insight into the Devol's world. She would know their secrets. A miracle had happened. From the thunderstorm, I met my girl again. We met the leader of Mohaba's forests, Alo. And now we had found Delorah, Mohabat's long lost sister, a Devol's family member. Finally, we could gain insight into our enemy's world. I felt closer to saving Mohaba from misery, at last.

I was buoyed with hope but Mohabat was alone inside Jewl with the Devols after her. I prepared Delorah, "Devols are finding Mohabat as we speak. She is your twin sister. She does not know you are her sister. Be careful how you break the news to her."

"Do not worry. I will not let Devols discover her. I know how far they are to reach her. I will get to her before they will."

"Look at me Delorah." I grabbed her arm. Her body spoke to me. I could tell she was not planning to deceive us.

"Let me go. Please. This is my chance to make things right. Do you trust me enough? Can I go now? Before it is too late?"

I freed Delorah's arm. "Alright, I am watching you carefully." My voice started to echo as Delorah headed back inside Jewl, "Remember, you will be rewarded if ..."

Delorah turns around and walks back towards me. She grabs both of my hands. She is the only woman other than Mohabat to have touched my hands. She rushed, "I have made up my mind. Please. Believe me, OK?" Delorah looked identical to Mohabat even in her black dress that covered her from head to toe. She rarely showed her face hiding behind her veiled cloth. I had to remove her veil to place my hands on her forehead. She had no time. She had to get back to Jewl.

Delorah looked at me and said, "I hope, Death, you know I am not evil. I took care of the creatures inside with love. I hid from the Devols to the best that I could." Delorah's eyes shined as she gazed into my eyes. Mohabat's eyes shine the same way. I found it hard to grasp that it was not Mohabat standing in front of me.

"We will see."

"You will see. I will bring her to you, I promise."

I felt content to see Delorah, a Devol, to have begun to side with us. We had found a friend, an ally, in the most unlikely being, a Devol. And even though Delorah felt dark like myself, a darkness forced on her by Devols, I could feel a new lightness enter her, my world and maybe Mohabat's.

"I am going to find the Devols before they find Mohabat."

"You will?"

"Yes, I will tell them that I shouted. I thought I had seen something."

"Alright, but what?"

"That Pretas were playing tricks on me," Delorah comforted me as she headed back with a plan into Jewl.

I walked back to my bowl. Delorah appeared at the fountain lake. She pretended to be feeding the animals. The two Devols slowly walked toward Delorah. One of the two Devol soldiers asked, "What is going on? We got worried about you hearing you shout. Did something happen?" I could not understand what the soldiers were uttering. I understood the conversation through Delorah's mind.

Delorah answered, "Everything is under control. Go on, you can go." The Devols became suspicious. Delorah further explained, "I was going to get more food. The Pretas frightened me appearing in front of the jars I was grabbing. I did not expect them to be there, that is all. See, you have nothing to be concerned. I have everything under control. Can you please go now? Let me do my job." The soldiers believed her. They luckily could not detect Mohabat's presence. They left and joined the other Devols.

By lending Mohabat my gown, I granted her invisibility. If I entered the room, the gown would return to me leaving Mohabat exposed. Mohabat had been visible to Delorah because they shared the same blood. After the Devols left, Delorah went to find Mohabat, while in shock. She feared I had abandoned her. She worried anxiously while waiting hidden behind the rocks. It would have been a matter of time before the vampire mermaid would have come after her if not the Devols. She could have been pulled into the shark-filled water. She could have become nonexistent.

Mohabat crawled down to hide behind the rocks. She huddled in a ball, trying to make herself as small as possible. She had been crying quietly by the time Delorah placed a hand on her shoulder. Mohabat jumped. She uttered, shaken, "I know you are a Devol trying to mess with my mind. Or, you would have harmed me by now. You want to torture me before destroying me, go ahead."

"No." Delorah had not seen Mohabat this close before. She recalls her familiar face but not as her twin sister. Delorah never had problems talking. She tried to gain strength to tell Mohabat the truth. She had found out about their past only a few minutes before. She knew it would be difficult for an Angelious to believe her own sister would be a Devol.

"You do not have to show yourself to me. You are a Devol, that is good enough for me … make it short."

"Please let me …" Delorah paused distracted by Mohabat's resemblance to her, then finished, "explain."

"What is to explain? It is not funny to make yourself look like me. If you planned to scare me more, you have. Bravo to Devols, the Devols who ruined our town."

"No … listen to me." Delorah had no idea how to tell

a scared Mohabat everything she shockingly found out few minutes before her. She wished they were out in the forests somewhere nice rather than delivering her the news in a cursed dark scary setting.

For a second, Delorah became frozen in thoughts. Mohabat wakes her with her angered voice, "Listen to me you Devol …"

Apparently, Delorah had not been listening as she remained in her own thoughts. There had been so much information to absorb in such a short time. Delorah had to find the strength to tell Mohabat in a not-so-ideal setting. She interrupted without hearing Mohabat, "I cannot believe my own eyes. You reflect me. How could that be when we have been apart for such a long time?"

"What are you talking about? I am not following you." Mohabat slowly began to notice with the amount of time passing that she was not about to be killed, thrown into the lake, or beaten to death by the sharks.

Delorah continued with her own conversation, "Yes, I know. It was tough for me to inhale it all."

Mohabat frustrated, "Please, you evil Delorah woman. I am begging you now. Stop with the fooling."

"What, no? I am not trying to scare you."

"Sure, you must have done something to Mahboo. I do not know if talking to you is a good idea. Without him … I am nothing. You understand."

Delorah whispered, "I am not a Devol." She tried to grasp being beside her twin sister. Mohabat was a pure version of her. Delorah was the opposite version of her, dark and evil. She did not know what and how to convince Mohabat about their share of same blood. There was pressure to deliver the news, maturely. She had to break it to Mohabat softly. She felt the pressure, me, Death, watching.

Mohabat, shocked from what she was hearing Delorah say, "Sure you are not. I know a Devol when I see one. You cannot lie about what you are."

Delorah softened her voice and calmed down, "Well, I guess you could say I am kind of evil. Yes. But, hmmm, does it count at all to you if I say I do not want to be one. Is that better?"

"There is no 'kind of' in this world. You are either a Devol or not. It cannot be that complicated." Worried, Mohabat concentrated on getting her strength back from fear disabling her completely.

Looking around to be sure not to be heard by anyone, Delorah whispered, "I am not anymore. You need to believe me. There is no way you can get out of this place without my help." Delorah became impatient trying to empathize with Mohabat's situation. She struggled to control her evil Devol upbringing, "Now you can either agree to believe me or not. It is up to you."

Mohabat, confused more than ever, felt nervous again, "You are telling me to make this easier for both of our sakes. It is not working."

"I am not here to harm you." Delorah felt horrible, lacking skills of empathy. She tried hard to pretend she does. It seemed being a Devol had turned her into an insensitive, cold, and mean spirit who had to work hard to show care and love. These actions were foreign to her behavior and hard to display.

"Sure, you do not." Mohabat lost hope. There was no communication between her and me. She was with a Devol. She expected the worse picturing herself caged or worse destroyed.

"Well, hmmm, I do not want to startle you. How do I say this?"

"Say what?" Mohabat's fear arose. She waited to hear the worse about my wellbeing possibly imprisoned somewhere in Jewl like the other spirits. She regretted borrowing my gown more than ever.

"To be honest, this is all new to me. Um, how do I say this?"

"Say it and get it over with." Mohabat, worried how she would handle the news.

"Not sure why this is so hard." Delorah had only heard the news a few minutes ago. She took a moment to think while Mohabat became impatient.

"I am begging you to make it quick; if you are planning to lock me up here, if this is your trick, well done, go on, just do it, hurry up, all right. No need for sweet talks. We need to get this over with already."

Delorah tried another tack. "Mahboo, as you call him. I know him, too, only I know him as Death."

Mohabat's eyes widened. "What? I do not think so. Mahboo would never acquaint himself with a Devol thief like you. Never." Scared of the Devols, she fought to keep her voice down. She felt an unfamiliar jealousy towards Delorah talking about me to her.

"He does not remember me. He and I have met in the past. I knew that he has been in love with someone better than me. Now I see it clearly. That it is you."

The defiance in Mohabat turned to concern. "Did you kill him? Please tell me. I am a warrior. He and I are not together. We are here to destroy you Devols."

"Of course not. If I destroyed Death, then I would destroy the world. I am not stupid. There would then be no one to keep the circle of life going."

Mohabat, relieved, "At least, you are a wise Devol."

"At least, as wise as you."

"I am not convinced. If you were, you would have never sided with Devols. You know how dangerous they are."

"I have heard many stories from the creatures here at Jewl. Believe it or not, I am not a Devol. I am their prisoner."

Mohabat, not convinced, took a moment to think. She moved her gaze towards the dark wooden ceilings. She almost became distracted wondering how she could not see Jewl with slight dimming light shining through. After her silent response, Mohabat changed her gaze back to Delorah. Her resemblance and the fact that she was a Devol gave her shivers. She tried to control her fear. She denied Delorah, "I do not believe you."

"Well, you will. I know it is a long story. You will. I am not here to hurt you. You can breathe now."

"Hmmm, I guess a Devol would not have this much of an advance in vocabulary to utter these words. I do not think they can hold a real conversation. You tell me that I can breathe now … is, to be honest with you, making me start to believe you, for some weird, awful reason." Mohabat said with doubts about changing her appeared spoken mind. Mohabat found it difficult believing anything a Devol would say. They are masters of deception. In Mohabat's mind, all the killings, brutality, and the cruel hyenas hurting their people never could be forgotten nor forgiven.

"I am happy to see our long discussion is finally helping." Delorah seemed to speak in such a way that sounded deceitful and scary. She was raised this way.

Mohabat looked puzzled. She took a moment to breathe in and out. "Alright, then tell me what it is that you are so eager to share." She stared into Delorah's eyes but soon moved her gaze more towards her lips. She could not bear looking at almost her own self. It creeped her out.

"I have been waiting for a miracle to free me from the Devols' grasp. Here you are. You are that miracle." Delorah said with a happy face. She had finally gotten Mohabat's full attention.

"Slow down, I have not quite agreed to trust you. I am glad to hear you are on Mohaba's side although you do not look, feel or appear like one of us." Mohabat felt stronger to look at Delorah's while she told her this.

Delorah sighed, "Yes, I do not but in my heart, I do. How do I say this to you?"

"Say what? Go on, you can tell me."

"I did not know myself either. I just found out. You know …"

Mohabat impatiently interrupts, "Know what? Tell me. Does it have something to do with how we look alike?"

"Yes, it does," Delorah released her groaned voice.

Mohabat created an answer in her mind. She began interrogating Delorah, "Did Devols force you to deceive Mahboo? Made you look like me? You can confess to me; I am not here to harm you."

"I do not think they have ever met Mahboo. Only I know about him, I think."

"Only you? I find that hard to believe."

"Well, they do know there is Death. They do not know his powers or identity."

"That now makes more sense." Mohabat began to feel less fearful. Her nerves began to calm down. She found it difficult to look back at Delorah. She avoided it as much as she could by constantly finding distractions like watching a weird flying creature or Pretas passing by. She found many excuses to talk to Delorah without her eyes catching hers.

"I think I can see him because he has allowed you to see him."

"You are not making sense now. He sees me but what does that have to do with seeing you?"

"I better tell you."

Mohabat's frustration began to boil over, "Tell me what?" She asked with an angry face.

"I am your twin sister."

"What? No. This cannot be true. That is not what I have been told about my past. You are lying, bluffing but why?"

Delorah did not anticipate further interrogation and doubts from Mohabat. She tried to be more understanding than she has ever been before. As a Devol, Delorah did not need to tolerate patience. Everyone listened to her orders. Delorah calmed herself. She promised Mohabat, "I am not lying. I did not know myself. I found out from Death. He started to talk to me as if I was you."

"Oh, did he?

"Aha, he did. It was amazing."

"I am sure it was," Mohabat sarcastically responded.

Delorah stopped. She feared Mohabat was not going to hear her nor believe. She was not used to anyone not agreeing or listening to her. Delorah had just found out that she did not own a Devol soul. She needed her own time to grasp this shocking news. Her life was about to change. She had to keep her promise to Death. That was the only way she could get help moving away and far from the Devols herself. She took a deep breath and tried to calmly explain to Mohabat, "He looked at my past life stories with his hands on my forehead. These bubbles above my head showed up and in them, all the scenes from my past appeared."

"So, he did ... hah?"

Delorah confirmed, "Yes, I have nothing to hide."

"If you are my twin sister, then why were you not with me when I was placed on earth?"

"You and I were placed in different places. Sadly, we were found by two different organisms."

"Oh, and?"

"And you got found by Death. I was not as lucky. The Devols, who soon discovered my gifted immortal soul, found me. They raised me to believe they are my family. I did not know any better until now. I am relieved, to be honest."

"I have always felt a part of me missing. I could not quite explain it. Now, it makes sense."

"So, you do believe me?"

"Well, you have said things about Death that no one else would know unless you did encounter him. So, yes Delorah, I am starting to believe your story."

Mohabat pretended to believe Delorah. She tried to believe her words although in a state of shock to make any right decisions. She looks around Jewl and at the far room's ceilings. She wondered how her enemy could be her own blood. She could not deny that Delorah looked like her. She tried to sound cheerful, "Then you must be my twin sister. No, I think identical twin sister. We do look quite alike, do we not?"

Delorah's face became happy. She nodded, "Yes, we do."

Mohabat did not relax. She went back to interrogating Delorah, "If you possess a good soul, how did you not notice sooner?"

"I have been helping Devols because I did as I was told. No one can question them."

"That is sadly true, they are horrible." Mohabat was not fully convinced yet.

"Yes, I am afraid of them. I did not know what they would do if I tried to leave them, or where I would go. Is it possible to hide from them?"

Mohabat, seemingly interested, "Keep going, I am listening." Mohabat brushed off Delorah's questions. She had no clue about Devol's powers. That is what she tried to find out by entering Jewl. She wanted to gain insight about them. She did not feel comfortable to share with Delorah, a Devol being, until she was confident that she was to be trusted.

Mohabat listened. She continued, "I have lost count of the number of times when I had to hide from the brutality happening all around me. It is unbearable at times. I could not understand how I could be part of it." Grief took over Delorah. She wished she had been Mohabat instead.

Mohabat felt Delorah to be genuine. She comforted her, "It was not your fault. You have told me enough for me to start believing you, I think."

"You have no idea how happy it makes me to hear you say that. We can be great sisters together. Lots to catch up on."

"Well, I am positive there will be plenty of time after the war for that. You need to know that if you do side with us, we can help you, but only after you have helped us."

"I understand completely." Delorah did not anticipate receiving kind reactions from Mohabat. She had not been used to it. Devols were aggressive parents. They ordered her and worse, used her all the time. She began to feel part of a team now.

Out of nowhere, serious Mohabat suddenly became friendly. She shared with Delorah, "I wish we were not in this mess. I could have taken you to the forest to meet my friends." Her identical sister instincts unconsciously took over.

"You know right now, I do not feel like I have earned my place. Let me help you rid Mohaba of these Devols first." Delorah brought the focus back to their battle plan. It helped Mohabat trust her more. She somehow portrayed similar behavioral traits like her. Her dark Devol outfit, attitude, and upbringing could not hide her true personality. Mohabat took this as a sign of hope. She allowed her fears to quickly fade. "Now that I have met you, I believe we can defeat them. We needed someone from Devols in our team, I cannot believe my own sister."

"I hope you know Mohabat, I never sided with them. I pretended I did just to protect myself. I could not escape them without fearing to be locked in Jewl like these other poor souls here."

"I now understand."

"You do?"

"Yes, I cannot imagine what it has been like to be in your shoes. I too have lived in fear of the Devols. Not in such close quarters."

I became relieved to see a friendship developing. I felt the missing pieces of the puzzle falling into place. Mohabat had a comrade with whom she could fight her way out. She would not feel so alone.

I left briefly to attend to an emergency in Russia. It took me only a short while as a gang fight seemingly dangerous turned out to be not. When I returned, Delorah was still talking to Mohabat. The silence that usually surrounded Mohabat now had become filled with chatter.

I listened to Delorah talking to Mohabat, "It has been unbearable. I finally managed to convince the Devols I should stay in Jewl. Told them it was needed to prevent the souls from escaping. I replaced a cruel Devol who abused all the creatures in his charge. I have been kind to a lot of the souls here."

"To the Pretas too?"

"No, of course not. I cannot make them like me. To them, I am their enemy who they need to seek their revenge to free themselves. They believe I am their enemy. I cannot convince them otherwise. Truthfully, I did not have the time to change their minds about me."

"I see."

"I know the many creatures here do not like me but you know Mohabat...I am sure they will help us in every way possible."

"I am confident when the time comes, they will. We all want Mohaba to return to what it used to be—a peaceful happy place. You would not recall how wonderful because you were with the Devols."

Delorah sighed, "I do not, actually, I have only heard ...

but yes, them planning to destroy anything good. I had to go along."

"I promise after all this is over, you will be welcomed in our town."

"I hope so. I want to earn my place there."

"Who knows, it might happen sooner that you know."

"I promise you that I am not after Mahboo. He is yours." Delorah became overwhelmed with love for Mohabat. She had not received any care from anyone before. The fact that she looked identical to her may have awakened something kind inside her which was missing for decades. They both knew there would be plenty of time to bond after the battle in Jewl is won.

Mohabat had forgotten about me listening in. "Gosh, me and Mahboo. I have never thought that he and I would ever end up together. Our powers clash. Did you know if I stay too long with him, I can vanish?"

"I am confident there is a way if you want it to happen. Look at us. Who knew we would ever find our way back to each other?"

"That is true." I heard Mohabat say and with that, my doubts melted. I identified she feels the same way about me.

"I am happy we have found each other. I am frightened of what they will do to you if they discover you have sided with us."

"You know at this point, so close to freedom, I am willing to take the risk."

"Is Mahboo watching us? I am certain he can warn us

ahead of time. He can read my mind, and yours, since you have mentally sided with us. Oh. I can hear Mahboo. Can you hear him saying hi to you?"

"I can. I cannot speak loudly or the Devols would hear. That is why I have been muttering this whole time."

"I think Mahboo just said he needs to talk to you and the Buddha."

"Buddha? No, you mean the actual Buddha from long ago? Why would he want to talk to me?"

"Yes, well … you are on our team now. All right? So, believe it from now on." Mohabat placed her hands on Delorah's shoulders as if she was one of her friends. This time, Mohabat did not hesitate to stare into Delorah's eyes while talking to her. "We will help you heal from the trauma you have endured. Hopefully, we can return your peaceful inner self to you."

Delorah, in tears, "I wish I could stop these tears. I feel relieved. Thank you for this, for believing in me. I know it is not easy to trust me right now. I am sorry for my past terrible doings."

"Do not be sorry. What happened was not your fault. Now we need to get to work. You must teach me everything before you see Buddha in case I should take your place, we need to make sure we copy each other's moves well. We look identical. Hopefully, no one will be able to tell the difference."

"I am glad they cannot see you. Hopefully, no need. If you become visible for whatever reason, then they will. Um, you will need to know how to act like me. Are you certain you can handle the pressure? They have no heart."

I decided it was time to break into their conversation. "Delorah and Mohabat, listen to me. Please be careful. We do not have much time. So much is at stake. I am happy for your reunion. When the time is right, we will have a feast. But right now, we have work to do."

Delorah and Mohabat nodded to each other. They cautiously emerged from behind the rocks, checking there were no enemies in the area. Delorah gave Mohabat a tour of Jewl. She did not know what Devols were afraid of, the secret that could destroy Jewl. Devols had never shared such important matters with Delorah. Delorah could teach Mohabat every other aspect of Jewl.

They explored the mansion, Mohabat and Delorah began to attract unfamiliar spirits. The presence of the two of them together seemed to be awakening new souls. They could not sense Mohabat's presence. The spirits were drawn to the aura of the twins. They entered a new chamber. Mohabat became entranced by the furnishings. They did not notice a tapestry hanging on the wall. When the women rested beneath it, a snake came to life. It bared its teeth and began uncoiling towards them. I shouted, "Delorah, Mohabat. Watch out, behind you."

Mohabat responded immediately. She struck a martial art pose and then waited until the snake moved closer. She struck the snake, knocking it unconscious. Understanding that anything could be helpful in destroying the Devols, she pulled out her necklace. It had a tiny jar hanging from it. She extracted the venom from the snake into the jar. She and Delorah continued their exploration of Jewl. Mohabat left the snake alive. I feared it would not give up its evil mission. I killed it and transformed it into a harmless rat within an instant.

The walls of the next room Delorah and Mohabat entered were covered in tapestries. The women did not linger. They continued to the next room which was filled with mirrors. They felt overwhelmed and worse, a sense of curse coming from the mirrors. They both could not see the door to the next room. As they felt their way around the room looking for an exit, a large animal rose from the floor and began to fly around the room. The creature hovered over them. It bared pointed teeth at Delorah and Mohabat. It began to move towards Delorah, ready to clamp its huge jaws on her. Mohabat looked powerless to do anything. Delorah screamed.

My view of the room had been blocked by the huge creature. I could not let it destroy Delorah, or let the Devols find Mohabat when they responded to the shouts. So, I transformed myself into a fighting bear. I soon identified that I was fighting with a spirit. I turned its soul into a horse. I then threw its soul into a hanged carpet. It became an image in a rug.

I dispatched the bear by the time when we heard Devols calling out Delorah's name. They had nowhere to hide and no time to escape. As I had feared, my gown got drawn back to me, leaving Mohabat completely visible. I tried to grab

Mohabat and bring her into the gown with me but before I could, Delorah, out of fear, pushed her into one of the mirrors. When the Devols arrived in the mirror room, all they saw is Delorah standing alone in the middle of the room.

Devols were annoyed with Delorah's behavior. It had been the second time that day they responded to her shouting aloud. They suggested she leaves Jewl for a couple of days. They arranged for another Devol to watch Jewl. Delorah followed the Devols out of the room, she quickly looked back. She saw Mohabat in the mirror, despair etched on her face, alongside two other mirrors that each contained a solitary soul. Mohabat did not move out of fear of being discovered. Delorah, with no choice but to follow the Devols, left Mohabat alone in Jewl. And with her exit, we lost complete contact with Mohabat.

8

THE APPLE ON THE TREE

Mohabat and her everlasting spirit became trapped in the mirror in a dark place full of evils. All forms of communications stopped. I made many attempts to save her. I failed miserably. I could not picture losing her. If I had to compare each soul to an apple, then I would choose Mohabat's from the tree. Of all the apples in the world, she would be the only one I would pick. Sadly, without my apple on the tree, our plans had to be suspended.

Mohabat's unexpected tragedy ruined all our foreseen plans. Delorah and her knowledge of Devols became our promising piece. Mohabat was like a ripe apple of my dream garden. Our destination was clear. We would both grow and blossom together. Now, our path to get there had become rife with tragedy. If it had not been for Mohabat, I would have gone back to my solitary life. All I could think of is that I could not abandon my life with Mohabat.

I could not give up on Mohabat. I had to figure out how to save her. I kept asking myself, and the universal gods, what Mohabat did to deserve this. It seemed unfair that she would not get to leave her mark on the town that she once was destined to rule.

I believed in universal intelligence having a part in this. That is why I felt more betrayed by them and the invisible gods. They had made a clear path for me to oversee the circle of life, a path that had been clear but demanding. Mohabat's road has been extremely challenging. I chastised myself for threatening her future.

It seemed clear to both of us what her destiny appeared to be. The opportunity for her to reach her potential had never arisen. I tried hard to help her reach her dream. Every time I tried to make things right, the opposite happened. I should have let Mohabat be. I could have figured out a way to defeat the Devols without her. I had gotten her into a mess that I did not know how to clean up without the risk of losing her.

Buddha taught me to be mentally strong. I failed him. I had once again been defeated. I pondered how I could be strong with Mohabat not under my wing. Buddha was right in noting that I focused too much on the future. He warned me many times, "The future is always unknown and unpredictable, Mahboo. You need to understand that what is known is only your present time. The past is the past and known. You can only learn from it." The only thing that I had power over is the present, however, painful it has been.

Buddha had cautioned me to live more in the present. He knew I am programmed to read people's pasts to determine their current and future transformations. I needed to separate my duty from my friendship with Mohabat. I focused excessively on my future of getting my desired apple alone in a garden full of passion. I longed from this for centuries. I created this secret garden for the two of us. Despite all I had created in the past, I suspected Buddha had been right. I did not know how to get my girl to a place of love. It seemed such a place is unknown to me as it was to her. For Mohabat's sake, I needed to focus on what is happening in the present.

Buddha had cautioned, "Mahboo, remember you need to separate yourself from humans. You think you can have the same dreams as they do. This is because you have tasted it when you raised Mohabat. I understand you. I was once human myself." But I had not been convinced that he understood me. Buddha told me to withhold the truth from Mohabat. I needed to tell her about our past. Now, I may never have the chance to.

When Buddha discovered me watching Mohabat every day, he pointed, "Mahboo, you need to let her go. She needs to live out her own destiny. If you decide to have the same dreams, you might not find your true happiness."

"But remember you told me there is a way. You told me that."

"You are a different engine, Mahboo. Your engine is not

designed to work with Mohabat's. I know you raised her. I know you think she should be part of your life. Have you ever thought about the fact that maybe by letting her go, you might find happiness?"

And now I realized him to be truthful. I should have listened to him. We had both thought Mohabat's fighting skills would help us in battle. But my focus on life after the battle, my dream of a life with her, had resulted in devastating consequences for her and Mohaba.

I did not have a hometown. Ever since Mohabat was placed in Mohaba, I discovered this town to be a sacred place. It turned out to be truer when Devols exposed hiding Jewl here. I wished for Mohabat to bring back many believers into our town after the Devol's defeat.

I wondered why things had gone so terribly wrong for Delorah. I had many questions. I went to my favorite cemetery to clear my mind. I needed to come up with a plan to save Mohabat. I needed to think.

I had so much anger in me. I longed for some light in my shadow existence. I am not supposed to exist; I am destined to be invisible. Mohabat had made me feel like I existed. I dared to dream of a garden full of apples without worms. I had seen many corpses and worms. They had become the backdrop to my life. For once, I had seen a promising light to my hollow world. I watch the dead. I smell the lifeless bodies six feet under. I feel peace in a cemetery. I feel belonged there. I watch over the corpses whose deaths I have smoothly carried out. This is my destiny— a life in a cemetery, not in paradise. If I walked in bare feet, I would attract all the worms. They would take over the entire garden until no room for Mohabat and me, and our friends, Buddha, Alo, and Delorah. The worms would destroy everything in life. My world should include insects, beetles, and worms. A life forms that is only gray and black.

The cemetery remained the best place to gather my thoughts. Like never, sadness enveloped in me. But I fought it. I could not give up and leave Mohabat in Jewl. I did not know how much time we had before Devols would take out what they were hiding inside. They would most likely burn the entire place down. I could not imagine Mohabat dying in the fire. If I did not save her, then the invisible gods would not save me from the pathetic gray man I had become. I needed to get her out and soon.

Until I could get Mohabat out of the mirror, I had no choice but to give up preparing for the battle. If Buddha disagreed with me, I would not join their battle team. We suffered a loss. We had to save Mohabat first before we could save our town. Mohaba suffered tremendously at the hands of the Devols, another day or two would not change anything for them.

The weather turned darker and a heavy rain began to fall. A dark cloud loomed over Mohaba. After sitting in the dark for hours, I left the cemetery to confront Delorah. She appeared busy; making sure everything would be all right with Mohabat not in Jewl. I waited by the same tree where I had my bowl full of water. I emptied the water. I could not face watching Mohabat stuck in a mirror. I saw Delorah come out of Jewl alone. For a second, I imagined it to be Mohabat. I could not help but to take out my despair on Delorah.

"Why did you push her into the mirror?" I sounded devastated.

"I had no choice, Mahboo. They were right there." Delorah tried to convince me.

"Do not call me by my name."

"You seem angry."

"Yes, why would I not be? She is inside a mirror, unreachable, thanks to you."

"I tried to save her. She is my sister. If they saw her, they would make her miserable and suffer. Would you have wanted that for her?" Delorah transformed from a relaxed calm state to an angry one. I had never seen Mohabat's face angry. To me, Delorah's identical look confused me. It was interesting to see the anger in Delorah but as if it was Mohabat's angry face. She had her black veil on. I could see her face through it.

"I was there, you think I would have let them? Why do you think I was there?"

"I know Devols way better than you, Mahboo."

"Sure, you do. I existed in this world before you put your feet in it. You do not think I know how." Delorah's comment offended me.

"Listen, stop being mad at me. I am trying to say that they are capable of many things. They possessed things inside Jewl that could make Mohabat vanish forever."

"It does not matter. I was about to make her invisible if you had not rushed to push her so eagerly. They would not have seen her if you had let me do my job."

"She is in the mirror, is she not?"

"Yes, but if anything happens to Jewl, she will be gone forever. See, you did not do us a favor. You destroyed our chances to go to battle. You sided with the Devols, now pretending to fool me. You are a Devol."

Delorah used my name again. "Mahboo, I know you are upset. I am too. We have to move forward and figure out how to get her out."

"You know I knew you were trouble from the moment I laid eyes on you. I knew you were contaminated with evil. Your soul is not pure. You have done many bad things out of fear. You pushed Mohabat into the mirror. Maybe on purpose."

"How else am I to tell you I did it to protect her?" Delorah moved away and sat on a rock nearby. I did not move closer to her. Instead, I stood at the same place and continued our conversation.

Anger overtook me. Delorah's calmness worried me. She did not feel any rush to rescue Mohabat. It brought a lot of doubt and suspicion in me. "Well, how do I know that this was not a plan of yours all along?" I would have kept on if Delorah had not interrupted me.

"It was not. You would have known, would you not?"

"You are a Devol, anything can be expected from you."

"Listen, I know I had a crush on you a long time ago. I

tried to get close to you but now I know another woman possess your heart. Everything is different now. I did not do this on purpose, Mahboo, you must trust me on this. I am her twin sister. I might be able to help you all."

"I do not know what to think anymore. You? Crush on me? All I know is that you are trouble. Look at how much problems you have caused us in Jewl."

"Mahboo, please."

I was mad and interrupted her, "Do not call me by my name. Only people close to me are allowed."

"Hear me out. I beg you. We need to move forward. Right now, all I am certain of is that you can help purify me. I am not begging you. I am saying … maybe, there is a way to get Mohabat out of the mirror."

"I am not convinced to trust you anymore."

"Listen, if we focus on helping me gain my soul back to its purity, maybe it will help Mohabat get out of the mirror."

With a strong tone of anger in my voice, I responded, "The mirror had been empty when you pushed her into. There are two other souls who are sisters in there. They have never been able to get themselves out of the mirror, never."

"Please, I think there is a way."

"I do not trust you."

"OK, I am willing to become identical to Mohabat. If you push me in there, I can bring her out. I know about the mirrors. I can ask my family more about its tricks. They trust me. They will tell me."

"Well, I guess I should stop thinking of you as the old

Delorah. I hope that you have changed. I am giving you one chance. One chance. Do not cross me or you will regret it."

"Great, I promise I will not." Delorah got up and stepped forward. She felt safe to stand near me again.

"We have to take you to see Buddha. I have to make sure Devols do not find out anything."

"They have allowed me to have a couple of days away from Jewl. I will talk to them about the mirrors. I will pretend it is possible they could escape, see if they can tell me any of its secret."

"Alright. Tell them you need time away from Mohaba to have a good rest from all the pressure. Something that will not make them doubt you, OK?"

"I am confident they will not mind. They think my work in Jewl is not that valuable anyway. I HAVE never meant anything to them. They used me and are still using me."

"You can stay with Buddha. These two days are not going to be easy. He may have you do difficult tasks to force the evil out of you."

"I am willing to do anything as it is needed."

"To be safe, tell them you may take more than a couple of days as you are not sure where you are heading … how much time off you need. They can expect you back soon."

"They have no choice. They think I am going to jeopardize their existence. They, themselves, suggested I take time off from Jewl."

"It is unfortunate that Mohabat did not get to have you in her life earlier when she felt so lonely here."

"I know."

"It is not too late if Buddha can help you. You have to be mindful that you may never return to them."

"I would love it if you could help me never return to these evils. They stole my right to be an Angelious. I will do anything to seek my revenge. I will help Mohabat out of the mirror first and um … if I get to be stuck in the mirror, then so be it."

"I guess I have no choice but to believe you for now. There are no other options. I would not normally trust you. I hope you know that. You are lucky to have this one last chance."

"I will not let you down."

"I have to believe you for now that you did not intentionally push Mohabat into the mirror souls."

"I am glad. I will not let you down, promise."

"Anyway, they have a way of tracking you. Once you are back to your original self, then you will be completely like Mohabat. They probably will not be able to see or feel you. Remember, you may never return as Delorah. You are sure about this?"

"Yes, very. I cannot wait for the day I am not their slave anymore. I am finished with being their victim. Just like everyone else is here."

"I sense you are being truthful. You must understand that I will doubt you until this is all over. I do apologize if it seems that I am blaming you for what happened to Mohabat. For now, I will consider you did it with good intentions."

"Thank you. I will make up for pushing her without thinking."

"Well, as I said before. You got one more chance to prove yourself to us."

"I totally understand. You have every reason to doubt me. I get it. I hope that by committing myself to this journey of becoming close to purifying and join your fellow highnesses such as yourself, Mohabat and Buddha, I can become worthy of a soul that should have rightfully been mine long ago."

"I am sorry for what you have been through if it is true that what you did to Mohabat was unintentional."

"It was, I swear."

"Well, this is it. As I take you to see Buddha, you will begin to feel a sense of joy and freedom. Hopefully, you may not feel the pain at first. You must go through many difficult steps first. I am confident, your golden soul will prevail. I hope."

"I hope so too. I am ready." Delorah cheerfully said with tears of joy.

"Go and talk to them then. Do not show any reaction if you can. You are not going to see them again."

"I know how much is at stake. Do not worry."

"Well, let us see." I anxiously worried. Devols could maybe read Delorah. They may know she had contact with me or the outside. I increased my voice, "I will ask you one last time, Delorah, are you sure you want to go through with this?"

"Yes, I thought we discussed this. I am not going to think

about not returning. I am not sad to leave. I am quite content. I will hide my joy like nothing happened. They will not figure out a thing."

The first thing Delorah did upon entering Jewl is to check on Mohabat. Delorah tried to communicate with her but no success. Mohabat's eyes were closed. She seemed to be in a deep sleep. Delorah wrote on the mirror, "We will get you out, my sweet sister, I promise you."

I watched Delorah through my bowl.

Delorah approached the two Devols standing inside Jewl. They were not only the leaders of the group but Delorah's parents. She thought about all the centuries she had been fooled by them. They repelled her such that Delorah hoped this would be the last time she would set eyes on them. Delorah focused on how much she gained from knowing their secrets throughout the centuries. She was about to commit her whole existence ensuring Devols would be terminated.

Delorah brought her thoughts back to the task at hand. She noticed that she had lots of time in the future to live the life she was born to live. Delorah knew she would have way more time than the centuries they had stolen from her after the battle is over. She has found her real family and all she needed is to prove herself to both me and Mohabat. While watching her, I could sense the longing in Delorah. It was showing in her eyes how badly she wanted to be welcomed into our garden filled with plenty of apples and happy days. I hoped her parents would not discover her excitement.

"Would life ever exist after the sun burns everything into

dust? Who knows?" Delorah asked herself, "But at least, I am going to have lots of time to make up for my stolen past. If I pass the test with Buddha, I will choose my own destiny." It felt good to think she would finally have control over her own fate. It seemed this was her choice, at last. After their victory, Delorah thought of how wonderful it would be for her to make her own decisions. Freedom. She would not have to constantly live by the Devol's rules.

I had seen her past, and how Devols transformed Delorah into an immortal soul from her own death. The demons forced prisoners to tell them about Delorah's powers. They wanted to use her but so they had to deceive her. Many poisoned souls were shocked that something like this had happened. Some holy being awarded an immortal spirit. Devols were not supposed to have access to anything good. The only reason they could access Delorah had to do with them finding and raising her as their own child only to convert her to an immortal Devol. Delorah's thoughts filled up with hatred and resentment. She thought back to the day that they took her life while lying to her in her bed at Jewl.

During her human death, Devols locked Delorah in a room, which had blocked all forms of communication with even me. Therefore, I never had known about Delorah. If she had died anywhere else, I would have known about her. I would have taken her life. If I had been present, my attention would go on as her being a woman like Mohabat with an immortal soul with similar DNA. If I discovered Delorah then, I know things would have turned out differently for Mohaba.

Devols had lied to Delorah. They had led her to believe that the planning of her death was how it had always been for her entire family. They scheduled her death so that she would become immortal with the help of other prisoners. Devols were not immortal creatures. They were diseased souls that spread their darkness into Delorah. She had believed everything they had told her over the years. As she closed her eyes that day, a spell transformed her immortal spirit into something that would always remain visible to the Devols.

Delorah focused on the moment when she would have to say goodbye to the only life she had ever known. She knew she would always be identified as someone who has been Devol's daughter. But she had to leave behind her past as a blind victim to a forward world of infinite possibilities.

Delorah finally approached her family. She talked to her parents as if nothing had changed. She whispered to them, "I was in the mirror room. I felt a presence of some creatures inside there. I am worried that someone might have figured out a way to escape. I was going to watch out for them. Now that I am going away for a couple of days, I am concerned Papa."

Delorah's parents seemed confident that the mirror souls could never return from the glass. Delorah asked in worry, "Are you sure?" They responded in their strained human voices. "Of courrrssee weeh aaaure sureee sooweattaahhrt." Delorah understood that their voices were not made for human conversation. Their attempt to speak sounded more annoying than ever before. Delorah had tried to teach them to speak fluently. They never mastered the language. Eventually, she had given up correcting their pronunciation. Unlike most creatures inside the mansion, she became accustomed to the Devol's poor talking skills. She could understand pretty much anything they said.

Delorah listened to the Devols giving her the secrets of the mirror souls. She heard their nonsensical explanation. "The souls in the mirror can only be saved if someone immortal helps them. No one is willing to do that. No one wants to be stuck in the mirror to free another soul. No one. None of our captives possesses an eternal soul. We are not worried, my child. Neither should you be." Delorah had never noticed how unsettling her parent's voices sounded.

Devols reiterated that an immortal spirit could travel through the mirror. It would end up locked in the mirror. They also in caution, just in case, told Delorah her immortal spirit had become clouded by the evil beings inside Jewl. She would never be able to save any of them even if she tried. Delorah decided not to press her Devol family any further in case they suspected something. Their leading conversation about her trying to save the sister souls and how it would be futile worried us. It was time for her to leave.

Focusing on sounding normal, Delorah asked her parents if there is anything they wanted to tell her before she left. They said, forced, "Geeehttt eeehhhe rrresssst yooohhh eneed maiii shaayllddh. Weee hhhafe bigggg blllanz affftehr." Their last words she heard were, "My child, remember you can only be away from Jewl for a few days. We need you here and you know why. We cannot let these captured souls destroy us. We cannot risk having you away for more than a few days. We have big plans to tear down Jewl."

Delorah asked her parents, "So I am free to go?"

"My darlingggg … yeeeesszzz, gehtttt thhhheee ressszzttt yohhhh neeedttt butttttt youuhh undertan, weeeehhh neeeedttt yohrrrr reettteerrrn, downt you?" Their voices began to cause Delorah to shiver. She did her best to hide her disgust.

Delorah spoke her final words to her Devol parents, "Of course, I do Mama. Papa. Of course, I do. Yes. I will be back before you know it. I loovvvfffeee youuhhh."

Delorah did not love her Devol parents. She looked happy as she came out of Jewl with a grin on her face. At last, she escaped Devol's grasp. Delorah was buoyant. I could read off her that she felt victorious. She walked away from her life of deceit, abuse, and torture. No matter what challenges she would face in her new life, it would be better than what she would be leaving behind.

I wanted to comfort Delorah. It had not been easy for her to face the demons. She resembled Mohabat a lot. They were so similar that I had my parental and love feelings towards her like Mohabat. I controllably hid it. I knew she is not Mohabat. I identified her anticipation to burn down Jewl. I trusted Delorah would save her own trapped sister.

Together, Delorah and I, both dark creatures, went to see Buddha. I wanted to make sure she transforms smoothly. We needed her to be completely on our side. I feared her changing her heart. She could give out all our secrets away at any time if things do not go well.

I had not yet told Buddha about Delorah and the rush to purify her. I hesitated until last minute after dropping off Delorah to tell Buddha that Mohabat was trapped inside Jewl. I had a hard time telling him that the battle could not go ahead. While Delorah looked around Buddha's cave, I took him to a corner far from his entrance to his cave. I told him everything that happened in Jewl. It pained me and him that Devols prevailed without a fight.

9

THE MIRROR SISTER SOULS

At Jewl, the souls inside the mirror time-traveled. Mohabat was along two souls who were sisters. They hung next to each other on the wall. Before Mohabat joined, the two sisters had accidentally discovered the layers of the mirrors. They found if positioned at the right angles, they formed an eternal access to each spirit's life. If they closed their eyes and held each other's hands, they voyaged into their past or future.

Although it had not been the best time for Mohabat to consider her past, she was one step away. The time-traveling mirrors could allow her to find answers to her long-standing questions. All Mohabat had to do is to learn the mirror tricks. She would no more need to wait for the truth.

I prayed the Devols would not turn Mohabat back into a

human. They had access to all sorts of spells. They harassed it out of their supernatural captives. They had all the resources to destroy Mohabat if they discovered her in the mirror. I did not wish the lady and the apple of my dreams to end up dead, broken or rotten. Although it is my duty to take lives, it is also my duty to save lives. I can enter a body with my own soul. I can rescue humans who are not destined to die. I cannot rescue a soul trapped inside a glass. I cannot give an immortal soul back to Mohabat, not if it is a golden one. Her spirit stuck in a crystal could be broken at any time.

As frantic as I was, I recalled that I had Delorah. While Mohabat appeared to me as a freshly picked apple, crisp and healthy, Delorah seemed the exact opposite. I felt her soul to be like an apple that was worm-infested and rotten. But Buddha and I decided to banish the evil out of her soul.

I had not broken the news about Mohabat to the Angelious. They passionately practiced battling and searching for the spy. I found relief in watching their high spirits. I did not want to dampen their mood. Nonetheless, I had a hard time carrying on. I normally enjoyed silence but missed Mohabat's presence with her team. She awakened feelings and memories that I had not known existed. My future would be empty without her.

Not knowing what else to do, I went to watch a funeral of the soul that I had taken moments earlier. I sat through the ceremony at the funeral home. I followed the family to the cemetery. This was something I had never done before. And throughout the ceremony, I grieved unabashedly alongside the family of the deceased. No one could see me. As the casket lowered into the grave, I watched it. I feared this to be Mohabat's future if discovered. Perhaps, the Devols would turn her into a human then kill her and take her soul.

I knew Devols were capable of anything. I convinced myself that after they take what they needed from Jewl, they would burn the place down. Mohabat would burn in her mirror. I would be unable to retrieve her soul. Or, Mohaba would be in misery taken over by the Devols.

After leaving the funeral ceremony, I went to watch Jewl. I stood hidden in a nearby tree. Jewl was standing. It was not on fire. This meant we still had time to rescue Mohabat. I suspected that the Devols would not destroy Jewl before Delorah returned. Through the water in my bowl, I observed Mohabat standing inside the mirror in a deep sleep. Not until later that I found out Mohabat had traveled back in time. What she discovered had left her feeling betrayed by me.

Mohabat had seen glimpses of her early death. Tragically, she had seen specific moments out of context. She witnessed how I sentenced her to a life of an Angelious. I later found out how she traveled into her past. She stood beside her own past young self. The other mirror sisters too vanished into their own pasts. After her death, she could not contact humans. She blamed me for taking her life.

A monkey dragon with hollow bones wished I would be in a better condition hearing from it what happened inside the mirrors. The creature had observed Mohabat for a while. It did not plan to startle her. I could understand why. Instead, it withheld from revealing itself to her right away. The creature told me that it wanted to wait for the right time to introduce itself. It told me, "I identified a lot of fear in her. It worried me. I feared she would think I belonged to the Devols."

The creature faced me as it spoke to me. It balanced back and forth with enormous bulk wings in the air. It stood few inches away from me with its face exactly same height distance from mine. Its wings stood noticeable against its small monkey facial features. It sometimes landed on the ground. Its big wings shrunk when it began to appear more as a monkey when walking on the ground. It climbed around the walls at times. Fire sometimes came out of its mouth. It shared the story of Mohabat and the mirrors. "I continuously observed her. I did not take my eyes off her. I soon began to be curious about her fascinating and yet complicated life story."

"I bet you did," I observed the dragon monkey's extraordinary features. It distracted me. I could picture us fighting the Devols together. Its strength combined with my powers would make us extremely powerful.

"Mohabat began to think that a Devol was first playing with her mind. After a while, it slowly became clear to her that it was her own past she kept seeing."

"I did not know there could exist such a thing as traveling through time. I can see human's pasts but never could visit the future or the past. It is an extraordinary experience, I bet."

The dragon monkey continued its mirror adventure story, "Mohabat seemed irritable. I guess, what is the right word? Oh, aha … ambivalent."

"That is right. For a small and I guess big creature like you, not designed for human speech, I am impressed by your language skills."

"Thank you. I think I learned from the two sister souls. To be truthful, not sure, actually."

"Well, it does not matter. Does it now?"

"Not really. But good I can speak with you and communicate. It should matter somewhat to you then, right?"

"That is correct. You are clever. I did not imagine monkeys to be so intelligent other than climbing around a lot. Sorry, I did not mean to offend you. I meant to complement all your extraordinary skills."

"I know. Anyway, let me continue what happened. I do not think she had been locked up before. It seemed the idea of not knowing how to get out, feeling trapped, slowly began to destroy her and her mind." The creature talked to me for hours. It expressed its reflections to me, "While I watched her, I thought about how lucky she was to not be human. Otherwise, she would have starved to death without food and water."

"She is lucky."

Through the creature, I found that Mohabat had seen the night she was to marry the powerful man she did not love. The plan had never been for her to marry that man, to begin with. I knew where the creature's story was leading. As much as I did not want to hear it, as much as it pained me, I let the storyteller continue.

While the creature talked, I daydreamed at times. I imagined Mohabat lying on a grass, the wind blowing leaves over her. A leaf landed on her face. She remained still, making no attempt to move it away. The wind lifted the leaf. It took it off to its next landing spot. Mohabat did not move with no life. I was reminded that in the thousands of years since she died, I never held the courage to visit her grave. I preferred to think she was there in Mohaba. I did not need to visit her grave. I watched her as an Angelious. She existed. But as the creature spoke, I made plans to visit Mohabat's grave to have a connection with her.

I did not want the dragon monkey to stop. I did wish for the clock to stop. While it continued her story about what had befallen Mohabat, I thought of the leaves falling in Mohaba with no one there to clean them up. I began to understand, and accept, that Mohabat is gone. It disturbed me to learn through another being what she experienced.

The creature described in detail how Mohabat journeyed in time. From the mirror, she watched her past unfold like a scene from a movie. She traveled to a moment in her past where she found herself sitting on a chair in front of a mirror. Behind her, a woman stood seemingly combing her hair. "Old, somewhat overweight, and short, standing behind Mohabat." The woman prepared Mohabat for the night of her wedding. She did not seem like a typical maid. The creature had taken its time to figure out from the conversation that the woman was disguised as me, Death.

It is true. I resurrected the body of a dying woman to get close to Mohabat. I remember the day of her wedding well. I advised Mohabat how important it was to go through with the wedding—a fake one. I promised her that I had everything under control. I swore that after the wedding, we would be together. But as she looked back on that day, Mohabat did not discover that the wedding was a sham. It dawned on her that the old maid, encouraging her to go through with the wedding, was me. After that, it seemed Mohabat's outrage at my deceit began to grow. She felt she had seen enough from her past to think of me as her enemy.

From her imprisonment in the mirror in Jewl, it appeared to Mohabat that I forced her to marry Mohaba's king. In fact, Mohabat did not see that the wedding was her own suggestion as part of our plan to destroy this evil man. It was her plan to get within his sights. She wanted to make the king fall in love with her. Our plan worked. But as the wedding drew near, Mohabat lost her nerve. She began to regret the whole plan. I remember the number of times she repeated to me, "Weddings are holy, not the time to mess with the Devil."

It looked to the mirror Mohabat that I seduced her to assist me with my plot to kill the king. A man whom invisible gods had not scheduled to die. Looking back to her wedding and my part in it, she believed I played god. Worse, I used her to assist in the killing of a man whom universal powers had not scheduled to die.

Before Mohabat could explore her past further, she got called back to the present by the return of the sisters from their journey in time. "The three of them were again no more than bodies stuck in the glass." The creature took a break when it noticed me listening with anger as I controlled my rage. It asked for my permission to continue. I wanted it to tell me everything. The monkey carried on as I instructed. "After returning from her past, in her frustration, she screamed loudly. The mirrors created an extra layer of glass instantly to protect against breaking. With no success, Mohabat gave up shouting."

"Go on, do not stop now."

"Fine, but please stop me if you need to. Well, Mohabat recognized the hopelessness of her situation. She was feeling betrayed. I could see she was upset. She had put all her trust in you. I think she feared being used by you to get what you wanted."

"Used by me?" I tried to calm myself down. I sighed. I then slowly gained my normal voice back. "What happened next?"

"While standing in the mirror, gazing at the empty dark room, her mind began to wander. She began talking to herself."

"Did you hear what she said?" I was curious.

"Well, I do not recall exactly. She could not see everything that happened. She had lots of questions."

"What kinds of questions?"

"Well, I think about how someone who raised her selflessly could use her in a selfish way." The creature stopped and looked at me.

I composed myself. "You can continue. What else?"

"She wondered if you would use her again if she ever gets out."

"I see, well I guess I would. Did she have any contact with the other two souls inside that mirror?"

"She did not at first. It was only after she started to give up hope of ever escaping that, yes, she began …"

"Hmmm … it must have been tough."

"Are you certain you want me to go on?"

"Yes, yes, I do. Go on."

"Alright then, she paid attention to the other sisters. They said to her that mirrors could take them anywhere in time."

"If that was the case, then why could she not see her entire past? I mean, that is what she wanted and requested from the mirrors to do, did she not?"

"Well, all I can think of is that she probably needed a strong mind, Mahboo, to travel. She was hurt and weak. The sisters warned her that she could get lost on the way and never return. Maybe that is why she did not get a chance to, you know."

"Oh, the sisters said that? Well then, I guess …"

"Yes, the sisters told her that it is not something she should take lightly. They advised her it had taken them a long time to figure it all out. They shared with her that initially, they traveled slowly. They did it carefully in time and returned quickly. They became more confident in their abilities over time with lots of practice."

"Yes, I mean they had plenty of time and bored with nothing else to do."

"True, for them, they shared with Mohabat that it took lots of patience. They apparently mastered their ability to travel further in time, gradually but slowly."

"I see. So, that is why she did not see her entire past."

"Yes, she did hope to find the mental strength to go into the future. She wanted to see if you abandoned her. She worried you had some part in locking her into the mirror."

It hurt that Mohabat thought I would let her down. She had known we were going to battle with evils of Mohaba. I was not the killer she imagined me to be. She began to suspect our friend, Buddha, is in fact, me in disguise deceiving her.

The creature did not stop there. "Mohabat suspected you abandoned her to be with her Devol sister, Delorah. Am I, right? Is that her name?"

I sighed, "Yehhhs."

"Good. Well, I could sense she was beginning to lose control of her senses. She sometimes screamed loudly in attempts to vent her anger."

"What about the sister souls? Did they try to comfort her at all?"

"They did not say anything. They understood her misery. They had been through the same experience when they were first trapped in the mirror. It was Mohabat, herself, who finally decided she needed to accept the situation. Rather than ignoring the sisters, she became their friend. She began to accept her fate, I guess."

"I am glad at least she had contact with other souls. She was not alone. She also had you, right?"

"Yes, that is right. At first, her madness frightened me. But when I noticed she planned to become friends with the sister souls, I recognized she had become ready to meet me. One night, while the sisters were sleeping, I was able to get her attention."

"Mohabat must have been extremely scared to see you? Even the bravest of souls would be frightened of a flying monkey with Dracula-like fangs. Sorry to be this honest."

"No, that's OK. It is true. I mean, at first, she was frightened. She said, 'If you are to take my immortal soul, then please do it quickly.' She thought I was a Devol sent by you to hurt her."

"She always seems to phrase the same thing when she is near death. She asks it to be done quickly. That is Mohabat all right. But good you were not there to take her life."

"Yes, I convinced her that I was not going to. I told her I appeared from the dreams of the two sisters. After Mohabat calmed down, I revealed my name, Neyolah, to her. I guess she knew Devols had no names maybe that is why she believed me."

"Good then."

"And then I told her that she should not accept her new fate. She would need to do everything she can to escape."

"Did she listen to you?"

"Well, I knew she continued to be scared. I kept talking as she got used to me. I advised her to not become consumed by her emotions. I could tell she had emotionally given up. Eventually, she summoned enough strength to respond."

"What did she say?"

"She shared her fears with me. She was upset that she had been betrayed and left to suffer. She seemed a bit distracted by the sight of me flying around. Eventually, I asked her if she wanted to be free again. She showed interest. I continued circling around her but minimizing her fear."

"I am surprised she trusted you quickly. It could be because you did not take her life but cared for her. You gave her plenty of advice. That is good."

"Yes, that was my intention. I know I am scary. I am a female dragon with monkey features. I do not think a male one would be as caring and sensitive."

"True, you have feminine characteristics. It is good. I am masculine but believe it or not, when I raised Mohabat, I began to learn from her emotions, good or bad, painful, or beautiful, it is what life is. Not death. I cared for Mohabat. I learned a great deal from her about life. Before her, I was an emotionless robot machine."

"Yes. I am not confident which one I am. Anyway, I advised Mohabat that she should not be giving up on her first day. If there had been a way into the mirror, there must be a way out." Neyolah stopped. It then stopped moving its wings. Her distance from the ground was not much. It fell and landed smoothly on the ground.

I thought about Neyolah's comment. She had made a good point. I observed Neyolah who began climbing around the room. It seemed that I had to switch from talking to a dragon to a monkey now. I responded to Neyolah, "Good, glad."

"She then questioned that if it were true, why the sisters had not been able to escape? I answered, 'Unless they are saved by someone who willingly gives up their immortal life in return, there will be no way that they can be saved.'"

"That is true. How did you know that is how it is supposed to work?"

"I had found out through the sisters' dreams."

"You can enter their dreams?"

"Yes, only because of the mirrors."

"I see."

"Anyway, Mohabat thought about what I had said for a moment, I saw a glimmer of hope in her eyes. She then asked me why the sisters had not been able to escape since their souls were immortal. I explained that they were witches and a witch's soul is different. Witches can live many lives. And their older sister had stolen an immortal soul. She used it to help her sisters re-incarnate for many centuries."

I did not anticipate a flying monkey to be as wise as it had proven itself to be. "I am glad to hear Neyolah that you became friends. You were there to help relieve Mohabat's suffering. Thank you."

"Yes, but listen. I am not finished yet. She asked me if the sisters could not use their powers as witches to escape the mirrors. I did not think such a spell existed. If it did, their sister would have saved them."

I thought about what she had said. "Perhaps it is because they cannot communicate with the outside."

"True. I told Mohabat I was created to find an escape for the sisters."

"Is that so?"

"Yes, I was supposed to fly away and find a spell for them, a spell to break the power of the mirrors."

"Interesting, and …"

Neyolah looked at me with wonder, then her voice changed. "I told Mohabat I had seen her dream about a powerful man named Mahboo—and that she cared deeply for this man. She was startled to learn I could read her dreams. She told me no one was supposed to know about you and that she could get into a lot of trouble for revealing your identity. I told her not to worry. I exist as a figment of the sisters' imagination."

"Oh Mohabat, even when she daunted me, she tried to protect me. I named her Mohabat for a reason."

"You did? What does her name mean?"

"It is an ancient word for kindness."

"Wow, she was kind that is for sure, oh, and, sweet."

"Yes, she was. But, anyway, I mean, unless she took the sisters into her memory, they would not know who I am, right?"

Neyolah's voice softened, "Hard to say, to be honest with you. Mohabat seemed protective of you. I promised her secret would be safe with me."

"Glad, you were there to calm her."

"Yes, she finally was able to relax a bit. She treated me like a friend and someone she can trust. I promised I would not abandon her but in case anything was to happen, I asked her if she thought you would be planning to free her."

"How did she respond?"

"She seemed confused. She strongly believed you deceived her. She was quite certain you were with her twin sister, Delorah."

"I know, she and her twin sister are identical. I sometimes mistake the two. I am Death and still can mistake the two."

"Crazy, but yes, they do look identical. It is scary, you do not find that scary?"

"Not really. I am Death; I am not scared of anything or anyone."

"That is right, of course, you would not be."

Imagining Mohabat in pain upset me. I probed Neyolah, "Were you able to help her at all?"

"I guess, somewhat, I did."

"What do you mean by somewhat?"

"I told her that if she wanted, I could enter her dreams to look for clues while she could watch. She agreed. That is when I actually saw her smile for the first time since she got trapped in the mirror."

"That is good, her smiling. What else?"

"Once she knew there was hope, she relaxed."

"Good." I became less upset at picturing her sad in there.

"She asked me about my teeth. I said I have no idea why the sisters imagined me with teeth like this."

"You do have funny teeth."

"I know, I said to her I wondered why the sister souls

imagined me as a flying monkey. And you will be happy to know, Mahboo, we actually laughed together."

"Great, at least she had some good time. You are unique. There are no flying monkeys that exist, you are imaginary. Good, Mohabat did not think she had lost her mind."

"Funny, Mahboo."

"Sorry, there is nothing funny to this. Carry on."

"I made sure she knows that I do not have any urges to bite anyone with my teeth or drink their blood. I did say maybe my teeth would be useful if something or someone tried to destroy me one day."

"Is that so?"

"Not sure, actually. She told me she was happy I was there with her. I said I would stay with her if I could. We would have to see what happens when the sisters wake up if I would still be in Mohabat's mirror."

"And ..."

"I believe I was created from their dreams."

"I see." I had to be present at other places. I postponed it to hear all the details of what took place inside the mirrors.

Neyolah told me that as Mohabat waited for the sisters to wake up, she got pulled into another dream from her past. This time, Neyolah was present with her. It went flying around the forests searching for clues. It eavesdropped on conversations to help Mohabat. She managed to get a glimpse of a moment from Mohabat's childhood when she used to be a toddler. She was wrapped in a bright yellow blanket surrounded by friendly animals in the forest who seemed to adore her.

I remembered that day as if it was yesterday. I had on an old robe and brown sandals. I wore a black cape. I had a rare black diamond necklace. I have never removed this necklace. It is invisible but with me. We were not in Egypt but in the forests of Mohaba. I had just come back from Egypt to be with Mohabat. A fox and a big dog were telling Mohabat a story about our past struggles with evil forms. Eagles flew overhead. Creatures and squirrels and birds flitted from branch to branch. The wind rustled the leaves in the trees. The skies were clear and sunny. These were the creatures that took care of Mohabat when I had to leave to attend to the demands of life and death.

The animals of the forest knew that universal gods brought them this magical baby to help save the entire universe. They spoke of how Mohabat's destiny would be to save Mohaba one day from evil. They somehow believed she would face evil but return Mohaba to the paradise it used to be.

I was glad to hear that Mohabat and Neyolah saw these happy moments from her childhood past. But the relief turned out to be short-lived. As Neyolah and Mohabat watched the idyllic scene, an evil soul entered the garden of reincarnation. All the animals fled in terror. I was left alone to deal with a demon.

I remember that day well. I had no choice but to take Mohabat with me to deal with the demons. She was too young to remember anything. Now, Neyolah told me they had seen everything in their time-travel. They saw me tell her to close her eyes. I placed her in a tree from where she could not see anything. Then, I took the evil soul and threw it into my instrument where it turned into a breakable ceramic vase. Next, I burned it to ashes to vanish its existence from the earth.

Neyolah articulated with disappointment, "Mohabat engrossed in the scene, she forgot about you."

"What do you mean? From me throwing the bodies into the instrument?"

"No, from me being suddenly pulled towards it."

"Really? Hmmm, I guess if you were there in the moment, that is possible. That is not good. Sorry Neyolah. No one is supposed to be there except the bodies and souls and me. I mean I took Mohabat there because I had to."

"After that, I ended up powerless against the invisible force. In a flash, I was lost from the scene and disappeared from the mirrors."

"Poor Mohabat." I covered my face with both hands. It was difficult hearing what she experienced inside the mirrors. I removed my hands from my face and placed them back down. I looked at Neyolah to continue speaking.

"It was a terrible experience."

"I can only imagine what Mohabat must have gone through after she lost you—alone again in the mirror, without hope or the will to live. And what happened to you? How did you survive? There is no possibility of re-births for imaginary creatures like you?"

"To this day, I do not know how. I ended up in Mohaba's forests where I found my children, alone and almost starving. What is incredible is I did not know I had children."

"It is incredible."

"I am surprised about Mohabat as an Angelious. She is supposed to have a protective soul. How were the mirrors able to pull her in? That is unthinkable." Neyolah went to attend to its baby dragon monkeys. I did not learn as much as I had hoped.

10

THE TREE WITCH LADY AND THE HESHMATS

Before meeting Neyolah and discovering what happened to Mohabat, I tried to get her out. All I could think about as the clock continued ticking was how to face a seemingly impossible situation. Cleansing Delorah's soul occupied Buddha, a risky business at best. I did not plan to distract him. We desperately needed Delorah to recover her soul. I had little time to figure out how to save Mohabat. I tried to see if I could find a spell that would do the job. Much of what happened inside Jewl seemed to be the result of spells. So, it made sense to seek out a witch whom I had heard practiced fortune telling.

I had identified the witch to possess special powers. I

never approached her. I feared her ability to discover who I am. She possessed enough skills to have kept her alive for centuries. The old woman apparently had built herself a unique tree house where she confidently hid all her treasures. Only people with special powers were permitted to visit her. Everyone else who approached her tree experienced curse. Even though she lived in seclusion, she fully seemed aware of the world and its politics, unlike many of Mohaba's residents.

I approached the witch's lair cautiously. I knocked on her door. A curtain at the window next to the door moved. I saw the crone eyeing me with suspicion. But the door did not open. I kept on knocking. And she did not answer. I smelled her fear beyond an anticipation of rage. I talked to her through her door.

"Dear tree lady, I know what you are thinking. You are thinking I am here to take your life. You probably know who I am. I am here as honestly as I can be. I have never exposed nor revealed myself to strangers. If I were here to take your life, you would not see me."

The assured the witch opened the door. She asked me to take my gown off and leave it on a tree branch. I complied with her request. She complained she could not see it. I explained it as my protective cloak and therefore invisible. Standing at her door, she asked, "Why are you here? You can do anything you wish with your deathly powers. Why do you visit me?"

I lowered my voice in case there were any creatures listening. "I am here because I need your help. I believe you possess skills that are strange to me. I have lost a dear friend to the mirror souls. I need your help to get her out."

"Mirror souls. I cannot help you there."

"Why?"

"I lost my two sisters, the Heshmats, to the mirror."

"I am terribly sorry to hear that but maybe we can help each other then. What do you say? You can save your sisters and I will save my friend."

The witch answered me, "This is difficult for me. I have tried everything possible. All the spells in the world did not work. They show up here sometimes. They spend time in the forest with me, but they cannot talk to me. They are either ghosts or I guess in a deep sleep, perhaps."

I worried about getting exposed without my gown. "Please let me in. We need to talk in private. I do not want to be unprotected, please. I am asking you kindly to let me in."

"Alright, but I have no spells for you to use. I have tried everything to save my two Heshmats. I can use my fortune-telling skills if you like. That is all I can do for you."

"Sure. If you find a spell later, I am fine with that." At last, the tree fortune teller lady stepped back. She let me enter. Looking me up and down, she said, "So, you are the Death that everyone talks about. No one has seen?"

"Yes, that is me. I am not at all what you think. I do not go after people and kill. I take lives as my duty to the gods of universe who created me to manage the circle of life."

"I do not believe you are Death then. You know how many

people die in the world every second? It is impossible for you to manage. It is impossible."

"I understand your skepticism. But you do not know much about me. I have existed since the beginning of time. I am the first with my given power. I then took animal's souls and evolved as they did."

"That does not explain anything."

"Please let me finish. Over time, I have advanced that it is all done automatically. I have a garden of violins where the dying soul goes to be transformed into its next life without my presence."

"You make it sound so simple. I have worked hard to connect with other spirits. You make it sound easy."

"You can either believe me or not. It is up to you. I only attend to situations where something abnormal is happening. I can make it appear as a normal death even though it is not. We have a lot of that happening in Mohaba. You can connect with me on some level with this, I am guessing."

"I guess that is true. Some of the creatures in Mohaba do not exist anywhere else in the world."

"Exactly. That is when I have to make it look all normal."

"Alright, if I say I believe you. Now, what?"

"Well, I am a being of my own, too. I exist because of my Death soul. I can separate myself from those responsibilities if I wish. So, here I am."

The witch began to soften. "I have to make a confession. I have heard rumors that an immortal soul can save my sisters."

"That is accurate. I found that out recently."

She seemed quiet for a moment. She shared with a reduced tone, "I feel I must tell you something. I am the crow who tried to steal Mohabat. I wanted to use her immortal soul to save my sisters."

Her confession took me by surprise. I had not anticipated her knowing about Mohabat. "How did you know she has an immortal soul?"

She answered guiltily, "I overheard you in the forest."

"Aha …so you are the creature who has been spying on me."

The fortune teller spoke in fear. She made her voice sound heavier to cover her shaky voice. "I earned my immortal soul through many centuries of practicing witchcraft. I have earned it," she declared defiantly.

"You could have used your own soul to get them out? Let me guess. You fear to lose your immortality or, being stuck in that mirror yourself for who knows how long?"

"Yes, I am afraid I could lose all that I have worked hard toward for such a long time."

I reacted, "Well, Mohabat is an immortal woman stuck in that mirror. I have no idea how to get her out."

"I cannot help you. I do not know how myself. If you ever find a way, then maybe I can help to save both Mohabat and my sisters without losing my own spirit."

I had not known that the witch had an immortal soul. I always believed she existed solely by practicing witchcraft, including casting spells. I delved, "You know how to tell fortunes, do you not?" The witch responded with interest, "Yeeehs."

It became clear to me that the tree lady needed an accomplice to perform her ritual fortune telling. I could read her mind but remained silent.

"I definitely can help you with that."

11

THE ASURA DRAGON MONKEY

The witch motioned for me to sit down. She pointed to a small round wooden table. We sat down on wooden chairs. The witch lady took my hands. She closed her eyes. I said nothing, waiting for what happens next. I began to relax in the quiet meditative atmosphere of the room. The witch's eyes flew open. She stared at a spot just over my right shoulder.

I slowly turned around. Right behind me, I noticed a creature that looked like a cross between a monkey and a dragon with huge black eyes and pointed teeth. Large feathers protruded from its back. It bared its vampire teeth as it landed on my right shoulder. I did not fear. The Heshmat lady shouted and fell backward against the wall of her home. In the stunned silence, the monkey began to speak.

"I am here because you asked for me."

I asked, "Who are you? I know all the creatures in this world. This cannot be real. You cannot be real."

"I am real all right. Have you ever considered that you do not know me because you never tried to look for me?"

"You do not fit the description of any creatures I know of. I cannot believe you are real. This cannot be. You must be a fragment of our imagination. Or, we are losing our minds."

The witch picked up a pan in her left hand with which she tried to hit the creature's head. But the pan passed right through it. The witch, fearing for her life, ran outside, and disappeared into the forest.

I stayed calm and said to the creature, "You are not of a physical form. Hmmm, how interesting. I would have awarded you a soul. I do not recall seeing anything like you."

The male creature left my shoulder and hovered over the table. He said to me, "You will understand one day. All I can tell you at this moment is that I am sent by the mirror souls."

"What? Mirror souls. No, that cannot be. I thought they had no powers or ways of communicating. My good friend, Mohabat, is trapped there. I came to the witch in the hope of finding a way to free her. Can you communicate with her?"

"No, when the time is right, you will discover. I am like you, living my destiny."

"Could you not tell me now? If you know something, please tell me. I do not have much time left."

"I am here because you were asking about your future. I suspect I am from the mirror soul's dreams. I think they saved me from the Devols through their dream. Time will tell. All I know is that they can dream. Anything in their dreams becomes real. I suspect I am one of their creations."

"Tell me about the future then."

"My presence is to show you that in your future, there will be many souls of different forms. You seem to have many enemies."

"I know. They are all part of the Devol's group. I do not think anyone knows who I am. How can they hate me if they know nothing about me?"

"In the forest, there are some Angelious and other life forms that have formed their own groups against you. Their goal is to destroy you. They think you have sided with the beasts. You might be battling with the Angelious. Who knows what tomorrow will bring? Many uncertainties. Anything can be changed, even the future."

"My presence is to warn you. To tell you that you need to prepare. If not, those whom you once loved may turn against you. It may not be the Devols themselves. You have to be cautious."

"I am pleased you are not here to hurt us. I am curious about what you are. Are you by any chance an Asura?"

"What is an Asura?"

"Let me tell you a little about the structure of the realm of all beings, if I may?"

"Certainly. I have been waiting to find out what I am, who I am and where I come from. So far, I have could only guess. My memory is lost."

"I am not entirely confident. We are like two different engines designed for two completely different purposes. Let me tell you more about this world of ours. In this world, we have many kinds of creatures and souls. You are evidence of one of them."

"An Asura?"

"Yes, I think. Asuras are known for their fighting abilities. You are destined to fight—I mean look at your teeth. They are designed for killing to add extra life to your own existence."

"It is true. Sometimes, I have the urge to draw blood. I prefer it to be of some beast that needs to be destroyed so its blood will give me the pleasure of victory."

"I have doubts about why you are a monkey, as well as a dragon. It may be so you can climb, as well as a fly which can be an extra fighting skill. You must have evolved this way. I may not have noticed your kind. Or, you do appear to be a spirit created through imagination."

"Maybe the mirror ladies created me through their dreams. When you were mentioning them to the witch I appeared, so …"

I felt confident the creature was not an enemy. I shared with it more about myself, "You might be right. I am not designed to kill spirits. I am designed to take lives of fleshly beings and put them through a re-incarnation tunnel. This might explain why I never knew you existed. I have nothing to do with spirits, like the Pretas who are hungry ghosts. They live their own destiny."

"Pretas, they sound scary."

I talked to the Asura for some time. Other than Mohabat, I had not spoken to someone for this long. Something came over me, I asked the Asura without a thought, "It has rather been an unexpected journey. Will you fight alongside me when I battle the Devols, or any bad Asuras, or who knows what else?"

"Of course. But, you know, we are guessing about whether I am a fighting spirit. I do know that I am male. I think I have been left behind from the dreams of the mirror souls. I will join you but if ever I should appear back in the mirror soul's dreams, I will vanish without warning. It could possibly happen in a middle of a battle. Will you be all right with that?"

"I think I can live with that possibility. Having you around if I can is better than nothing."

Joy took over the Asura. "If we are going to do battle together, then you will need to know my skills."

"I sure do. If you wish."

"Great. I create fire, which is useful if we want to destroy any evil forms. My fire does not destroy physical creatures. It can kill bad spirits, Devols, and beasts."

I moved my chair back, relaxing my legs. I said, while calm, "That is wonderful, beyond what I had hoped for."

"We do not know what kind of creatures the Devols have created. For all I know, they have created creatures that look like me. I got saved, before it was too late, from becoming a Devol. This is my conclusion based on my fragmented memory."

I agreed that he might be right.

The dragon monkey continued without stopping, "If the Devols have a fire, then they are fools. Fire will not destroy an Angelious or a spirit soul. We will have the advantage."

"But what about you? Can their fire destroy you?"

"They cannot if I am quick enough to turn invisible first. The trick is …

"What, please tell me?"

"I can at any time vanish."

I was impressed. "How?" I thought to myself. I was the only creature who had this ability.

"I can go back into the mirrors temporarily. It is not that hard to disappear. What might be the risk is me getting lost in the sister soul's dreams and not return."

"It is quite interesting. I am slowly understanding how you came about. I am not confident who the mirror souls are but, for now, I am content with having you help me in our long difficult journey."

The Asura dragon monkey looked cheerful. It asked with a happy voice, "Then what are we waiting for? Let us begin this journey."

For the first time in a long time, I felt hope. I had taken a risk coming to the witch, but my risk had paid off. I gained a new friend with whom I could talk and with whom I felt protected. I am Death but in a world of unknown creatures, I needed a friend and warrior of my own.

I began to think of more practical matters. The Asura was small enough to sit on my shoulder as we moved about. And it could hide underneath my gown if necessary. It looked small but when it spread its feathers, it appeared quite big and intimidating. And the fire that it could breathe out could turn anything nearby into ashes.

We needed to escape the claustrophobic atmosphere in the witch's home. The Asura and I went for a short walk in the forest. We chose a name for him. Together we came up with, "Hayoolah".

And so, began our friendship. I shared with Hayoolah everything that I shared with Buddha about my abilities, my life, and Mohabat.

Hearing about Mohabat, Hayoolah wondered, "I think Mohabat has something to do with the mirror souls. I am not sure why. I have a feeling I came into existence through the sister souls who dreamt about me."

I had to describe Mohabat to Hayoolah but then he interrupted me, "It does not matter. You know. I would not know anyhow. I never saw the mirror soul's faces. I was in their dreams a lot. I heard voices which appeared to be coming from the mirrors that had souls. But nothing else."

"Hayoolah, we should stop wondering about how and why. We must start accepting we met for a purpose. I have big plans for you, big plans."

Hayoolah pulled itself closer. It slowly transformed into a monkey with his dragon feathers hidden behind him. It took small steps to reach near the ground close to my chair. "We need to take what we have now ... using our powers together to destroy the Devols."

"We have to leave it to the gods, Hayoolah. There are many things unknown to me. We will prepare as much as we can and hope for the best." I identified a renewed hope within me. I had a new sense of direction. I was not alone anymore.

"I heard you mention big plans. How about if I let you sit on my back. Let me take you to the higher ups? After all, I am a dragon for a reason."

"I have flown before Hayoolah but I have not sat on a dragon before. Yes, we can go."

Hayoolah took me high into the sky from where we could see all of Mohaba. I spotted dark auras here and there throughout the town. There seemed to have been a cluster of them around Jewl. These were the Devols. From this vantage point, I could create a map of where the Devols hid. I knew it would be dangerous for both Hayoolah and me to expose ourselves to the Devols. They would know who their real enemies were. We decided to be invisible. We would be undercover but would wait until the day of the battle. There were so much more to discover and strategize over to save Mohabat but, with Hayoolah's presence and friendship, I could visualize our victory again. I realized that Hayoolah felt like one of my own kind. I decided to share more information with him.

"Hayoolah, I would like to introduce you to someone legendary who many believe has died. As you know, I know of all the existing souls on the planet. You shall promise to keep this secret between the three of us. You must promise that if you ever get called back by the mirrors, you will never tell.

He is a worthy soul who the universal gods and I awarded the ability to appear as a human form. He will live until the end of time."

"I am curious. Please who?"

"Well, thousands of years ago, the individual known as Buddha, awakened in enlightenment. His lifetime teachings involved meditation in search of internal happiness without any form of attachments to material things."

"How is he here now?"

"He exists because of his immortal soul. He is assisting many of our people in disguise. He has formed a strong group of monks."

"I cannot wait to meet with him. He can help me be enlightened."

"He is currently helping Mohabat's sister, Delorah. Devols stole her many years back. They ruthlessly abused her. Buddha is helping the sister regain her inner strength and return to her original destiny. We have predicted a couple of days for her recovery time. It is going to take longer to transform her back to her purity."

"It appears he is a perfect fit to return her peaceful soul back to life."

"I sure hope. I mean he has helped many reach their true happiness. I trust he will bring her back to her original self."

"I am curious. How does he aid you?"

"He and I are a perfect match when it comes to matters of the afterlife. Our interest is the same. We both care about the souls. Buddha gives me a lot of guidance. He understands me."

"I like this wise man. I am confused how I can be a good spirit fighter. I wonder if he can help me. I have this demon desire inside me. It is tempting. I do not trust myself."

"That is understandable. Buddha is sure to be of help to you. You do need to resolve your questions. He teaches per the spiritual capacity of each creature. I go to him for advice about many creatures."

"You are telling me all this because you plan to introduce him to me, is that right, Mahboo? Oh, and, you have not told me how he earned his eternity powers."

"Yes, well, I valued his loyal devotion to human souls' life. I made the call to award him his honorable soul. It is something that came naturally to me. I did not do it on my own, the gods of the universe with its powers helped me."

Hayoolah pondered, "What about his passing, how?"

"He was 80 years old. The invisible gods called me to take his life. When I reached for his soul and threw it into the tunnel of re-incarnation, he bounced back. To my surprise, it did not pass through the reincarnation."

Hayoolah flew back an inch and further up in the air. "No, really?"

"Yes, really. For the first time, ever, I saw a man earn an immortal soul. I made the choice to keep him the same way he has been as human. I did not attempt to pass him through the tunnel again. I sat with him. I told him about me and my powers. He was the first soul I opened up to."

"Why do you think he got awarded the immortal life aside from being a man of wisdom?"

"He seemed to be the enlightened one who did not fear death or being born into an animal world. This usually frightens humans who enter the cycle of life and death and re-birth."

"He must own one of the most powerful spirits. I will be honored to acquaint."

"Great, we have a tough journey ahead. Let us pray we find a way to save Mohabat before Jewl is gone."

"You know by now; I am at your command. Whatever you wish will be mine as well." Hayoolah lowered itself down to be closer to me.

"You have to promise me, Hayoolah, to never tell anyone without my permission. Anything that happens when we work together must remain between us. I mean it, between us ONLY."

"I am not confident that secrets you share will remain safe Mahboo. If under my control, yes. I promise not to say a thing."

"Good. That is what I needed to hear. The future is unpredictable, Hayoolah. One can never know how safe it is, my Asura." I looked at Hayoolah. From its eyes, I saw a future full of victories.

"I am glad to be at your service, Death, my Master."

I woke up from my daydream. "We will conquer lots together, my dear Asura, I have no doubts. Back to Buddha. I call him by his name. To his students, he is known as Ghavi."

"He sounds familiar. My memory is bad. I turned into a dragon monkey without knowing why. I have a feeling about it, you know. Weirdly, I have some memories, but not positive from where or whom."

Genuinely concerned for Hayoolah, "I usually can read any beings' past lives. For some reason, I cannot read yours. You probably have been modified somehow, which would explain why I cannot read you. Maybe one day, we can find out who you used to be."

"I hope. I would like that to happen. I am willing to help without this possibility of ever finding out. Destroying the Devols is enough justice for me. Maybe it is my destiny to be this creature forever by your side. You know what?"

"What?"

"Sometimes finding out about your past may force you into a situation where you feel obligated."

I felt Hayoolah. "That is right, I cannot agree more. I battle with this issue. I see the hurt in all those who have lost their loved ones. They do not know, one day, they will reincarnate into something else; completely detached from their previous life."

"They will not remember?"

"No, I do not believe they do. I am not certain why the invisible gods do not allow. I have thought about it. I trust if they know their past lives, that in the new form, they would not be free. To be honest, I have not figured out its purpose. I do not question the gods. I trust their logic."

Hayoolah content, circled in the air. Fire began to rise

inside its jaw. "Great minds think alike. So … you were telling me that Buddha exists. Are you planning to introduce me to him then?"

"Yes, I am. He can assist us. He will direct us in a lot of ways. As you have learned, he is stupendously wise. We need his leadership."

Hayoolah, overjoyed for the adventure, "We should go meet him then. What are we waiting for?"

"Wait, before we meet with Buddha, I like to tell you about a secret of mine. I think you can help me with."

And so, I told Hayoolah many of the unraveling events between Mohabat and me. I shared the details of why I could not be with Mohabat. My Death duties surpassing all other logics. "I created creatures to protect her. As you can tell, it was quite difficult for me to let go of Mohabat, to let go of the promises she and I made to each other long ago; extremely difficult," I sighed.

I told Asura how I raised Mohabat. I told him how I kept every piece of Mohabat's hair, which to me is like gold. I collected bits of her nails, dead skin, and a little bit of dried blood from her innocent bleeding. I thought if the day ever came that we could regain our powers over the Devols, and if anything happened to Mohabat, I might need a piece of Mohabat to use to bring her soul back to life. I had hidden the pieces of Mohabat's parts underneath rocks in the forest.

I collected bits of Delorah during our brief time in Jewl, which I hid behind a tapestry, for just the same purpose. I shared with Hayoolah not only my secret of the souls I programmed to protect Mohabat, but also the locations of the places I had hidden Mohabat's pieces. I taught him what to do if I were not there to save Mohabat. I wanted him to know where to find the pieces in case I would be unable to do it myself.

Hayoolah promised me to be my warrior partner and assisting Asura. He created thin fire, burning the small wooden wall with letters in a language that I did not understand. "Here, this is my written promise to you, Mahboo. To be at your command at all times."

It was a relief to have someone with whom to share the pressure of my duties. I had not recognized how heavy the pressures weighed on me until I acquainted with Hayoolah. I could picture defeating our enemy, with an Asura by my side.

I warned Hayoolah that what I was about to ask him to do would not be easy. Hayoolah seemed to understand. He moved his monkey looking face near me, "Mohabat is a blessing. She is stuck in an endless curse. Setting her free depends on one thing and one thing only: Eliminating the Devols. This will free her—and you."

12

HAYOOLAH AND BUDDHA AT BEHESHT

The time came to introduce Hayoolah to Buddha. Invisible Hayoolah perched on my shoulder. I gave details to Buddha and revealed the hidden Hayoolah. Buddha did not seem pleased. He dreaded I lost my mind. Buddha was convinced that I brought a Devol into his presence. I persuaded him to move closer. He took a good look at Hayoolah. His novelty drove him to softly touch his forehead. But when he did, his hand passed right through. I asked Hayoolah to create a fire, which he did, and, startled Buddha. He fell back to avoid the real flames that spewed from Hayoolah.

Buddha acknowledged this strange dragon-like creature. To be entirely doubtless that Hayoolah has no connection to the Devols, Buddha requested that I take him, remaining invisible, to a place near the Devols. It was true. We did need to find out what happens if he was placed in their presence.

Hayoolah and I approached Jewl. We spotted few monkeys on the ground with dragon-like wings. I hid Hayoolah underneath my gown. We were invisible. We inched closer to the monkeys. I read their souls. They were all spirits of creatures possessed by the Devols. Their darkness remained in sharp contrast to Hayoolah's pure spirit. I thought, "He must have been saved before contaminated by the Devols. He must have escaped before it was too late. Thank God he did."

Once I felt confident there were no connections between the Devols and Hayoolah, we retreated to a safe vantage point. We watched the other Asuras fly away in the dark cloud of their auras. Hayoolah cried, perhaps over the fate of his doomed fellow Asuras. It was too late to save them. I felt bad for Hayoolah who seemed lonely. I took him to my garden, Behesht. It is a beautiful refuge with many waterfalls. It has a large old tree known as the Tree of Life. Beautiful creatures flitted and pranced often around this paradise. I summoned Buddha and the Angels. Together, we gathered around the thick tree of life to pray.

As we prayed, Hayoolah's tears merged into a golden flower, which, carried on the breath of all our prayers. It entered Hayoolah's body through his wide jaw. The flower healed his internal wounds. It transformed him into an angelic spirit. The flower inside Hayoolah offered eternity. Its golden leaves would remain inside him until it would be time for other Asuras to be transformed. The ceremony transformed Hayoolah into a glowing happy monkey. The magical leaves offered him control over his destiny. This was unlike the other poor creatures wounded by the Devols. Never had he imagined he would be an angel, one of the worthiest souls in the universe.

After the ceremony, Buddha, dressed as a monk, approached Hayoolah. He draped a necklace around Hayoolah's neck. Four small pictures of Asuras decorated this bright brown necklace. Buddha whispered into Hayoolah's ears, "My dear Asura, stray strong, find courage with wisdom. Keep this necklace close to your heart always. Never take it off. It will guide you against danger." Buddha moved his hands and face away from Hayoolah. He turned to me and looked at both of us as he said, "This necklace will summon me when it is touched."

"Of course, Master," I kneeled.

Hayoolah went down on his knees, "I am grateful to you."

Buddha informed us that now an Angelious Hayoolah would not require any training. All his doubts about Hayoolah disappeared. He believed Hayoolah to be a unique creature with valuable powers. Buddha began to see in Hayoolah what I had recognized. He possessed powers that would be greatly needed in time of the battle. He encouraged Hayoolah to accompany me to the monks' practices, a sure sign of his trust.

While we were in Behesht, Buddha invited Hayoolah to enjoy the garden of paradise. He spoke with me in private first. I had been intrigued by the budding relationship between Buddha and Hayoolah, and the ceremony. So much so that I had forgotten about Buddha's quest to rehabilitate Delorah.

Buddha and I looked around to make sure no spirits eavesdropped. Buddha spoke guardedly, "I am sad to say, Mahboo, there has been no progress with Delorah."

"What?" I paused then apologized, "Sorry, I did not mean to be rude nor raise my voice. But I thought it was doable. I mean Delorah, she possesses an immortal soul. It is designed for an Angelious spirit, is it not?"

"Yes, it is Mahboo. What I do not understand is why you decided to save her right now?"

"Oh ...," I did not know how to respond. In shock, I answered Buddha, "I thought while she is away, it would be a great time to save her. But, you do know, she can help us with Mohabat."

"It is great that you are a hero, Mahboo, but sometimes you have to think about the battle ahead. We could have used her for the battle as a Devol. She could have helped while pretending she is one of them. Do you know how many souls we could have saved that way?"

"I understand but it may have been dangerous the other way around. I mean, look at what happened the first day she and Mohabat met in Jewl; a lot of the captives in there now blame her. To me, it seems more dangerous for Delorah to remain a Devol. You do not see in that way?"

"I am not confident, Mahboo. You might be right. It is difficult to determine right now. You do know right from wrong. This is our chosen path now. We must go along with it"

"Look at poor Mohabat trapped in Jewl. I fear the longer she is in the mirror, the more she is going to blame me for everything."

"You cannot be weak, Mahboo. You must remember my advice. You need to focus on the present. We have all been distracted by what happened. Without Mohabat, we are not going to battle."

"Yes, I understand, Master."

"Good, well then, we need to remain focused. That includes getting Delorah help. Make her an Angelious if you can, all right?"

"Yes, Master."

"We may never get Mohabat back. We need at least Delorah. I must be truthful, Mahboo. At this moment, Delorah is not ready. She is neither a Devol nor an Angelious. We may not have enough time. Do your best."

"But Master, you cannot demand me to stop worrying for Mohabat. I cannot give up. I will never give up until I save her. The thought of her not existing is killing me Master."

Buddha sighed, "I know Mahboo, I know. But, stay present. Try to be strong. My purpose is to wake you to what is at hand; the present. We can only live in the present. Yes, Mohabat is stuck in the mirror. Yes, she will be saved. I will make sure that happens."

"You will?"

"Of course, I will."

"You do understand how difficult this is for me. I must be reminded of Mohabat every single moment that I spend with Delorah. This is hard for me. I thought two days would be good enough to get the task done."

Buddha placed his right hand on his heart. "Oh, Mahboo ... how many times have I told you? You cannot think the way you do. Be strong even if it is for Mohabat. You are a hero. We are all here because of you, do not ever forget that. Stay strong in your mind, my friend. Think wise. Emotions sometimes fool us. Do not forget." Buddha slowly removed his hand away from his heart.

I nodded. "Yes, Master. I understand that getting Delorah the help she needs must override my selfish desire to be with Mohabat. I need to stay focused. I understand and yes, my emotions, I will keep them under control, promise."

Buddha relieved, "Great, after all, Mahboo, you know you are the one who wished to save Delorah. Finish what you have started my dear, dear friend."

When I heard Buddha repeat 'dear' to me, I identified the importance of the task at hand. "I shall do whatever it takes to save Mohaba and Mohabat. My Master," I paused for a moment then swore, "This is my promise to you and our town. You shall see."

"We cannot see tomorrow nor feel it. Stay focused. Be aware, your time with Delorah is becoming increasingly dangerous. Devols will soon start looking for her. It has been two days now. Be careful, my friend. Act quickly and again ..."

I interrupted Master. I anticipated what he would say. "Yes, Buddha, and again stay focused. I shall."

"Good Mahboo. I think my job is done. You are trained to handle this task."

For a moment, my mind was completely blocked. I forgot Master's last words. I continued the conversation, "I was wrong to think it would only take two days. I guess with all the centuries of mental abuse, torture and betrayals Delorah endured, it makes perfect sense. She has suffered more than any other creature. It has been centuries now that she has been with those beasts."

"Yes, it sadly has."

Without hearing Buddha's comment, I continued what came to my thoughts, "I must help her because she is Mohabat's identical twin."

"Exactly, my friend. So, you shall Mahboo. We cannot question what happened any longer. We cannot change the past. What we can do is act wisely in this moment. This will, indeed, help us change the direction of our future and save our town from its misery."

I nodded, "Yes, I understand it will."

"Alright, I am going to bring Delorah here."

"I will try my best, Master, to assist her in cleansing her soul. Behesht is a perfect setting."

Master stressed, "When you call for me next, I will be expecting an invitation to a ceremony; a ceremony to bestow on Delorah an Angelious soul. I see you as a hero, Mahboo. By helping others, in addition, and aside from your time of duty, is honorable. I am proud of your devotion to Mohaba, the universal gods, and Mohabat."

"Thank you, thank you, Master."

"No need to thank me, Mahboo. You cannot thank me when it is a fact. I am confident you will learn some lessons of your own in this path of cleansing a poisoned soul."

"Is this why you do not want to help her?"

Buddha waited, convinced by his own words. After a short break, he denies, "No, I think she will have a faster recovery here at Behesht."

"Are you positive, Master? I mean, I have seen you heal many before her in a short time. You do not believe …?"

Buddha stopped me from asking. He sighed, "I thought it would be easy, Mahboo. All right? She has an immortal soul. But she has suffered a great deal at the hands of the Devols. Her situation is complex. She may never be an Angelious. I think Behesht is a good healing place for her. The rest and her fate are not up to us, Mahboo. At the end, it is up to the higher gods."

"Well, if you see Behesht as the best place for her recovery, then so it must be. I regret that I have not spent much time here myself. We use this place mostly for ceremonies."

"I feel this place is the way I can see her heal, Mahboo. She needs to be in a healthy and peaceful place for some time. With me, it will take several months if not more. She needs to recover from her horrifying past. We do not have time. If anything happens in Jewl, we may lose Mohabat."

"We definitely cannot afford that. You do not believe I should be helping Mohabat right now and not Delorah?"

"I am going to do that now, Mahboo. Leave it with me. You tried. I know the dragon was brought to you. Truth is, it did not help you find anything like how to help save Mohabat out of the mirrors now, did it?"

I sighed. "No, it did not. But, if I had, um, had more time in the forest with Hayoolah, I may find out something."

Buddha firmly rejected my offer. "No. You had your chance."

"I know, I did. Well, are you going to stay with us at all or …?"

"Yes, I am. I will stay long enough to help Delorah under-stand our next plan. I do not hope to discourage her; that she is not progressing or feel that she has failed us."

"How are you going to find out how to save Mohabat?"

"Leave that to me."

"Please, please share with me your plan."

"Alright, we know an immortal being is needed to save her. I will turn myself into a creature of the forest. I will blend in with them for a while."

"I did not think of that. That is brilliant."

"Well, good you see it that way. In the meantime, you will be busy working on regaining Delorah's soul. Is that clearly understood, Mahboo?"

"Yes, I mean it is likely that we will need her to help us save Mohabat."

"I will spend time in the forest. I will listen to the rumors going around about Mohabat. After all, Mohabat has been appearing in the forest with the mirror sisters in her dreams. I might be able to communicate with her. I hope to save her before Delorah's ceremony."

"Are you certain you are safe? Will these creatures not find out you are immortal?"

"They will not, Mahboo. I have had this soul for thousands of years. I would not be Buddha if I were not wise in what I do."

"You are. I am happy to know you will be safe in the forest. I do not want to risk losing you. I am eager to help her; more now that I know her spirit could maybe save Mohabat."

Buddha grabbed my shoulder. He looked directly into my eyes while he continued to speak. "We will get Mohabat out of the mirror. With all our hard work, I promise you, we can. All right?" Buddha shook me gently, holding my shoulders tight with both of his hands. Once he let go, I was strongly convinced we were on the right path.

No matter how difficult, I had to focus on Delorah even though my heart focused on another. "I hope, I really hope Mohabat returns to us in good shape and health," I sighed with my voice softening.

"I might see her in the forest if she is in a dream there like the other sister souls you told me. If I find anything, I will call out to you, do not worry," Buddha grabbed me by my shoulders again. This time, harder.

I calmed down. "Please be cautious. May the gods protect

you!" This time, both Buddha and I had our hands placed on each other's shoulders. We had an unspoken act of oath.

"In good deeds, the gods will bless us, you will see with your own eyes, Mahboo. Keep up the good work, my friend."

"Are you positive, you will not require my assistance during this time?"

"Do not worry. I am immortal. I am protected from harm. Well, my friend, tough journey awaits us. We shall remain positive. We are moving towards victory and not defeat. Repeat that in your mind. Never let a negative thought come between you and your task of helping Delorah."

"I promise you, I will do my best."

"Good, we should bring Delorah here. Once we have a talk with her, I will leave."

We summoned Hayoolah. I secreted him under my gown. Buddha and I closed our eyes. We travelled instantly to Buddha's sacred place. We found Delorah placed in bed, sweating with fever—and exaggerated fear of Devols coming after her. Drops of black sweat dripped on the floor. They seeped into an underground pit containing a burning pyre. The sweat hissed. It evaporated as it hit the fire leaving no traces of the old Delorah. Buddha told me how to build such a fire at Behesht. We could continue the exorcism. He then wished Hayoolah, Delorah and I luck in our journey.

"We will reunite on the day of Delorah's ceremony. Hopefully, by then, our path will be much clearer. Goodbye, my friends, until I see you." And with that, Buddha was gone.

13

THE RACCOON AND
KANGAROO BEAR

Upon Hayoolah's and my departure, the witch, Matin Heshmat, returned home. The possibility of her sister's return made her glow. She had uncovered plenty of new secrets. With their return, Matin would advance her skills. They would never be deceived again. Also, no other creature would dare to trouble them again.

When Devols had discovered Matin's immortality, they put her witch sisters in the mirror to force her to give up her immortal soul. Matin refused to give it up under any condition, or for anyone. Her sisters were trapped. Even though she loved them dearly, it did not make her into a fool. She used her magic to see inside Jewl. She had noticed the third empty mirror next to those of her sisters. She informed me, "Death, I am too much of a risk. Demons are merciless, particularly unpredictable. If I had given up my soul, I would have been trapped with my sisters. They would not have freed them."

The creatures of the forest knew Matin well. She lived in an off-limits tree to everyone and had few old friends from her past lives who visited her at times. Any other creatures were discouraged from visiting, and any creature that tried to steal one of her spells was never seen again. Those who had never seen her imagined her as an old crone with a big nose. They envisioned her as someone who stayed locked in her tree house all day, practicing different spells.

What most of Mohaba's creatures did not know about Matin is her hidden social life outside of her tree house. With her immortal spirit, she often got visited by friends who were souls from her past lives. She found pleasure frolicking in the forest with them. But making spells were part of her skill set. Matin kept her Heshmat sisters alive for all the centuries by a protective spell she put on them. The spell did not break when the sisters got stuck in the mirrors. This meant that they could one day be saved.

I told Buddha about the existence of the witch. Buddha had known Matin but had never met her face to face. He also knew the location of Mohabat's cave. Master planned to disguise himself in the forest as an animal until he accidentally runs into Matin. He changed his plans at the last minute. He spent more time inside Mohabat's cave. After leaving

Behesht, disguised as a raccoon, he went straight to Moha-bat's cave.

Buddha quickly entered Mohabat's cave. He temporarily discarded his raccoon disguise. He searched through Moha-bat's things looking for clues. He discovered how Mohabat admired beauty in things that she had collected. He regretted the possibility that she might never return to enjoy them. Master disciplined himself to think positive thoughts. He allowed positive energy to enter his soul. "Mohabat will be saved," Buddha repeated over and over. After a long search, he came across an old painting of strange creatures he had never seen before. It grabbed his attention.

Buddha stared at the painting. One creature strikingly stood out baring its sharply pointed teeth. Master brought the frame closer to his face. As he did, he noticed another paint-ing hidden behind. He wiped away the dust to get a better look. And what he saw made him drop the painting. It landed on the ground in a shaft of sunlight. He held a picture of Hay-oolah wearing the necklace that he recently placed around his neck. Buddha pondered, "How could this be? I created the necklace not long ago and this painting is ancient old."

Master picked up the picture, hoping to find some answers. Perhaps the painting was a prophecy created years ago. In the painting, Hayoolah seemed to be flying. On the ground, three beings stood alongside one another. Their faces turned towards a ghostly female figure lady on a white horse with a spiraled horn on its forehead. To the left of the woman and the three creatures, to Buddha's greater surprise, was a familiar figure—a tall man dressed in a long black gown. It had to be me.

Master grasped that the three figures standing in a row were all familiar. The first one dressed in orange robes of a monk and most likely himself. The second being, wearing red with lots of black spots all over its gown reminded Buddha of Delorah. The final figure included a woman in robes of green and brown, possibly the tree witch. Buddha talked to himself, "Oh lord, three, must be symbols of Mohaba's immortal existence, and the ghostly figure on the white horse, Mohabat. It looks like Mohabat."

Buddha continued to stare at the painting. He sees a group of bats flying over his head and out of the cave. He watched them for a moment and then returned his attention to the painting. He decided that the time had come for him to visit the witch.

Buddha transformed himself back into a raccoon and shuffled off to the witch's tree house. As he approached her lair, he saw skeletons and animal skins hanging from branches. Many of the pelts were raccoons. He hesitated, frightened he too would end up hanging from a branch. About to retreat, he stopped. He thought, "Oh lord, Mahboo did not prepare me for this. I guess if it was dangerous, he would have warned me. Well, here I go. Stay positive. Focus."

Buddha hid the painting in Mohabat's caves. He made plans to show it to Matin if he managed to survive her initial attempt to destroy him with a spell. As soon as he approached her tree home, the witch detected his presence and looked out. She saw an approaching creature that looked like a raccoon. Matin transformed herself into a fox. As she crept up to the raccoon, she identified the presence of an immortal being. Matin raised her voice in question, "Who are you? Why would you dare come near my home when you clearly can see what has happened to others of your kind?"

"If you were a wise witch, you would know by now why I dare"

Heshmat circled around the raccoon. She spoke with saliva dripping on the ground. "I know you are immorhhhtallll, khwwweeeeyyy." Her voice came from a fox's throat. Heshmat lacked skills to talk through an animal. She rarely communicated while possessing a body.

Raccoon Buddha did not circle with the fox. He stood strong. "If you cared about the creatures around you, you would not need to be in hiding, creating all these spells to protect yourself."

The raccoon's strong energy did not allow the fox to near him any closer than five footsteps. Matin discovered his strength, "Are you here to teach me lessons about who I can and cannot be?"

"No, not at all ... I am not here to change you. I do not have the luxury of time to do that even if I wanted to save you from your miserable life."

"Oh, realllllliiiihhh. I am nooohttt in hiding. Not at all actualllliihhh." The fox thickened its throat to speak smoothly, "As you know, almost all creatures of Mohaba know exactly who I am and where I live. They do not dare come near my home."

"Well, let me remind you. You have not earned your immortal soul. Deep inside of you, you do know. You stole this soul from someone worthy centuries ago. Do you know the consequences of your terrible act?"

The fox continued to speak with more force to speak clearly. "Even if I did steal my soul, I am smart enough to win it over. I earned it. It is minnnneee." Again, Heshmat thickened its throat to speak with a controlled voice. "This soul is rightfully mine and mine forever."

"I see." Exhausted Buddha in a raccoon's body continued to move its gaze at the circling fox.

"There is nothing anyone can do to change that. I am here till eternity. There is nothing you can do about it, now is there? Why are you here anyway? To lecture me? I doubt it."

"Trust me, no … I am not here to argue. I do not have time to waste."

Matin grew tired of defending herself. "So, why are you here?"

"Mahboo sent me. Do you know him?"

"Yes, I met him recently. What does that have to do with anyone or you here?"

Buddha glanced around the nearby forest. He whispered quietly, "We need to talk in private."

Matin became curious, "Alright, but only because I know Mahboo … I will trust you are of the same kind."

"I am. I am. Now, can we go? You will know my identity

soon. I suggest we go to a safe place. I know somewhere we can talk away from prying eyes and listening ears."

The day turned to night. Buddha, disguised as a raccoon, and Matin headed to Mohabat's sacred cave. On the way, the witch picked up a piece of wood from the forest floor and, with a few words unrecognizable to Buddha, turned the wood into a torch to help them see their way through the forest. But the fire continued to grow into a lion fire containing Matin's spirit. And before long, the lion fire attracted unexpected guests.

The fire spirit woke fifteen indigenous spirit's attentions. They blocked Matin and Buddha with a torch. It had an angry bear emanating from its flame. The bear spirit faced off with Matin's lion. A fight was about to break out.

Buddha yelled, "Stop. Stop, right now. I mean it, right now. All of you. We are not each other's enemies … we are all sided with Mohabat and Mahboo."

Everything went quiet. Silence momentarily took over. The indigenous spirits turned their attention to the raccoon. The bear fire flew near Buddha. Master's powerful energy extinguished it from five footsteps away.

Alo asked the raccoon, "How did you do that? No being has ever turned off our fire souls before?" Buddha transformed himself into a monk and retorted, "It is my unconscious spirit; my internal battle skills."

"We worried Mohabat's cave was in danger; to be discovered by thieves and this witch of the forest presenting herself as a crow."

"It is all right, you can trust her."

"If you two are sent by Mahboo, I trust that your intentions are good. I do not feel any evil spirits present."

"Glad. Now that you know we are not here to steal anything, Mohabat is in terrible danger. She is locked in Jewl by the Devols."

"That is not great. We did not know that. We noticed she had not been here in the forest. May we aid you?"

Buddha took one step forward towards Alo and put his right hand on his right shoulder. "We will try to save her. We do need everyone's assistance. This means that all of Mohaba's forces have to come together, my friend."

Alo Hopi agreed. "We will do all we can. I am curious what brings you to her cave?"

Buddha paused for a moment. "I have discovered a painting in there. It seems to be a prophecy—or a clue as to how we can save her."

Alo stresses, "May I see this painting? I might be able to help."

Matin joined in the conversation. "Oh, now, I know. Therefore, you brought me here, is it not? Well, I would like to see this painting too."

"Yes, you will see it soon. I will be right back." Everyone followed the monk. Buddha stopped them and accentuated, "It is better you do not come in. You both possess powerful souls. This might wake some spirits inside. I would rather have them stay asleep. We have no time for distress."

Matin seemingly upset says to Buddha, "You mean me, don't you?"

"No Matin, I do not mean only you. Alo Hopi has a powerful spirit, also. He can wake a spirit not ready to be awakened, all right?" Buddha surveyed the group.

One of them spoke up. "Good, what are we waiting for then? We want to see this painting."

"Hmmm," Buddha took a moment and pondered, "I am worried the painting might be seen by other spirits. Alo, you must send your tribe away now. We will go to my place where we will be safer."

Matin anxiously said, "Are you certain that you want to trust me? I mean taking me to your place and all?"

"I am not concerned about our safety at this point. Right now, all I want is to help Mohabat. I was supposed to protect her. I have failed us both."

Matin kept thinking about her sisters and how all the trouble would help rescue them. "I will not tell a soul."

"We can worry about this later." Buddha placed his right arm on Alo's back. He quietly spoke to him, "Will you make sure that your tribe does not follow us?"

"Yes, of course." Alo turned around slowly. He faced the monk, "I will send them away right now."

Buddha nodded, "Thank you. May the gods bless you!"

Alo grinned. He was a spiritual man. It was his honor to encounter and work with powerful spirits. He walked towards his tribe and sent them away. He joined Buddha and

Matin. They waited for the tribe to leave before they headed towards Buddha's place.

The three spirits walked together. Buddha spoke to them in a whisper about the frame. "I have a strong feeling that it is a prophecy. I have seen present events in this old art. The frame is an ancient drawing."

"Is that possible?" Alo asked with wonder.

Matin went fervent, "I believe in prophecies. They do exist. Fortune telling is a form of prophecy."

"Well, there is a white horse with a spiral horn in it. I have never seen one."

"I have. It is a precious unique horse. If so, it needs protection. What I can offer you, Buddha, is an animal spirit. Please accept my gift." Alo took one step back. He called out for an animal. An enormous bear appeared, landing at his feet. It had features of a kangaroo, as well as a bear with a pocket big enough to carry a horse.

Alo looked directly at the monk Buddha while Matin cautiously hid behind a tree. "This is my gift to you, dear Buddha, from all the creatures of Mohaba's forest."

"How did you know I am Buddha?" Without saying a word, Alo communicated to Buddha, that he knew the monk's spiritual path since birth.

Matin interrupted, unaware of the mental communication channel that Alo had opened. Feeling safe, she walked towards them, "I never knew kangaroo bears existed. This is incredible."

Without any attention to Heshmat, Buddha spoke aloud to

Alo. He expressed his gratitude to him. "I am honored to know your gift is going to save not only Mohabat but everyone here in Mohaba. Now, I feel confident that we will make it. I can feel it. Thank you, graciously," Buddha grinned. "I am thanking you on behalf of all our monks here and the victims." Buddha turned slightly sad.

Alo acted the same as Buddha. He put his arm around his back to comfort. "You are welcome. This bear will protect you from danger. You can see, it has a kangaroo belly pocket. It is meant so you can hide. In fact, there is enough room for four spirits. No enemy will know you are there. They will only see a black bear if they see anything at all."

Matin looked unsure. "What about me?"

Alo gazed at her coldly. "You can also hide in there; although you do not possess a worthy soul. I pray you will be of help in our journey to save Mohabat."

Buddha broke in on the icy exchange. "We should not waste more time. Please come in."

The three spirits entered Buddha's cave with the bear spirit invisibly remaining in the forest. Matin investigated the room. "What a beautiful place you have. Look at the ceilings. I thought you lived in a simple cave. What a beautiful wooden statue. Too bad they are not voodoo dolls, hay? Look at these fighting tools and instruments. I did not expect you to possess all these things. I imagined you practicing meditation with no belongings?"

Buddha cut Matin's conversation short. "Let us focus on what is at hand, shall we?"

Alo resisted Buddha's comment. He complimented, "Well, your place is magical. It is exactly how I imagined it to be. But, yes, we shall focus on what is at hand. So, where is this painting that you have been telling us all day?"

Buddha acknowledging their admiration, responded to both Alo and Matin, "Thank you and thank you. Let me go and bring the picture."

Buddha left to retrieve the picture. Matin slowly whispered to Alo, "I feel terrible being here. I feel it is NOT my place."

Alo Hopi, trying to control his disgust for Matin, said with an undertone, "You do know it is not too late for you. If you start doing good deeds, you may be forgiven by all the creatures whose friends and family you have tortured and killed." Alo's voice thickened as he finished his last words.

"I have never been surrounded by good spirits. I do not like the Devols. I am not an enemy, you see. Ever since I became a witch, I have had no choice but to protect myself."

The indigenous Alo listened but remained dubious about Heshmat's sincerity. "Fair enough, but you did not need to kill the poor creatures to protect yourself now, did you really, Matin?"

At that moment, Buddha returned. Matin spared having to answer Alo.

Buddha held up the painting to make it easy for Alo and Matin to examine. "Here it is. I did hear you two talks, by the way. Before I show the picture, I have one last thing to say to Matin. You chose to be selfish. You selfishly hung on to an immortal soul that did not belong to you."

Matin's spirit flagged. "How have I become such a hated witch? After I lost my sisters, I felt empty with no purpose. I did lose my way. Seeing your place Buddha makes me want to be like you. Um, what is the right word ... enlightened?"

Buddha's tone softened. "It is never too late to change your path Matin, never. After I share this painting with you, I hope you begin to learn that maybe your sisters were stuck in the mirrors for a reason. Maybe the gods have plans for you. Maybe it is time to change your path and old ways with the new."

"You think?"

"I know so. Now that Mohabat is in there, it might be a sign that you are being given a second chance. If you help us and Mohabat is free, you might be recognized as Mohaba's savior. All the creatures will then forgive your sins."

After Buddha's inspiring words to Matin, the threesome focused on the image. Matin recognized Hayoolah, Death and herself in the painting. She guessed that the lady on the horse had to be Mohabat. She spotted her two sisters standing inside the mirrors on the wall. "This is the mirror room at Jewl where my sisters are locked. I am sure of it."

Alo added, "The horse has a spiraling horn. It is a unicorn. They are precious. There are few of them found in the world."

"A unicorn. So, that is what it is. Do you know what it can do? Where they can be found?" Buddha impatiently asked.

"Well, hmmm ... obviously, this picture is showing the

future. It is clear from the drawing of Mohabat that we need to find a unicorn."

"Well … we know we read someone with an immortal spirit; someone who can bring Mohabat back from the mirror but are there such things as an immortal unicorn?" Buddha asked Alo with wondered eyes.

"I believe all unicorns are immortal. The horn keeps them circle life without dying. I am guessing an immortal soul is required to jump into the mirror with the unicorn to draw Mohabat's soul out."

"Matin, Delorah—Mohabat's twin sister—and I are the three with the immortal souls shown in this painting. We have to be there at Jewl with the unicorn, Death, and Hay-oolah."

Matin wondered, "Who is going to give up their soul for Mohabat?"

"It is probably going to be one of us three or maybe the unicorn."

Alo jumped in, "We cannot worry about that right now. When the time is right, things will come into place. The kangaroo bear can hide all of you in its stretchy pocket. It can hide the big unicorn temporarily while you need to go inside Jewl."

Buddha confused, "Any ideas where we can find a unicorn?"

"I am hearing the whispering voices of the forest trees, outside. They are telling me where the unicorns can be found."

"They are?"

"Yes, give me a moment." Alo listened silently to the voices of the spirits. He then said, "They are found in the holiest places. Apparently, there is a garden of paradise where there is a Tree of Life. If we can get to one of these places, we can communicate with the tree souls, who then might direct us."

"I know such a place. It is Behesht. Mahboo and Delorah are there. They are working on helping Mohabat's sister, Delorah, to regain her true soul."

Matin spoke up. "I see. I am not allowed there, am I? I will not feel comfortable in a place where I am hated. I have doubts that I will be welcomed … so, we must see … I will await you in my home tree until you return with the kangaroo bear."

"That sounds like a good plan. Thank you, Matin, for your understanding. I do pray for your sisters to be sent back to you one day." Buddha looked sincere.

"I do not think that will happen. We will see, I guess. In the painting, they are in the mirrors. It does not show what will happen when we are all in the room. You better show up at my door, all right?"

Alo Hopi became agitated. "We better go. I am going to advise my tribe that I will not be around for a little while. My son will be leading in my absence."

Buddha and Alo prepared to leave for Behesht with the kangaroo bear spirit. Buddha knew Alo was an outstandingly worthy spirit. He belonged to be in Behesht with Mahboo,

Hayoolah and Delorah and him. Alo placed the painting in the bear spirit's pocket. He looked back at Buddha. Without a word said, they closed their eyes and moments later, opened their eyes to the calm garden of Behesht.

14

THE CEREMONY AND THE UNICORN SPIRIT

Buddha and Alo Hopi met with a beautiful sight in Behesht—a happy and healthy looking Delorah. Her time in Behesht had restored her eternal peace. Alo looked somewhat surprised to see Mohabat in the garden. The crisis appeared to have passed. He explored the garden and summoned the bear spirit. Taking the painting out of its pouch, he handed it to Buddha. "Goodbye Mohabat, Mahboo and dear friend. My work is done here."

Whereupon Buddha grabbed Alo's arm gently. "Please, do not leave. You only arrived."

"My work is done. Mohabat is right here, saved. I will go get my tribe ready for battle."

"She is not Mohabat. It is her twin sister, Delorah. I told you about her. We saved her from Devols in Jewl."

"Are you positive? I have never been wrong. Must she have the same immortal soul then? That is rare."

"They are identical sisters."

Alo stared at Delorah before relaxing. "Alright."

Buddha called out, "Delorah, Mahboo … hiiiiy. Come on here."

I greeted them. "You have returned. Does that mean you have found answers?" I stopped. Delorah remained silent.

Buddha responded firmly, "Yes, Alo and I think we have."

I noticed the strange black bear beside Alo, "Ohhh, what is this doing here?"

Alo looked at Buddha then moved his gaze towards me, "He is my gift to you. He will help you carry the unicorn to Jewl."

I grew puzzled. I looked to Buddha for clarification.

Master smiled, "Yes, a unicorn. I found this painting from Mohabat's cave. It seems to be a prophecy."

Without looking at the painting, I asked Master and Alo, "Who do you think painted this? The painter can tell us where to find a unicorn. I mean, I have never seen one, have you?"

Buddha responded, "I do not believe we have time to look for the painter. It is an old painting. The painter is long dead."

Alo continued Buddha's conversation, "It is clear from its texture the painting has been done centuries ago."

This is when I became curious about you and your painting. I wanted to know who you are. I did not have time then to learn much about you. I became fixated on the painting to see if I could figure out your soul. It had been difficult as the painting appeared centuries old. It meant that I had to spend a good amount of time researching you. I hoped to convince Buddha, "But maybe I can find it. Maybe I can read its entire past. How else are we going to know where to find a unicorn, right?"

Alo Hopi seemed certain he knew how. "I believe unicorns are a symbol of purity and grace. There will be a ceremony for Delorah, right?"

Buddha and I nodded. "Yes. We were waiting for your return. Since you are here now, we can begin our celebration of Delorah's regain of purity."

Delorah pondered, "What does that have to do with a unicorn?"

"Well, if I have understood, you are becoming holy again. Unicorns appear in the holiest of places. If we pray together for a unicorn to come to your ceremony, it might."

Buddha showed the painting to me. I did not disobey Master and Alo. I did not look for you then, Fatem. From your painting, it was evident what we needed to make the prophecy come true. We put our energy on making the unicorn appear. Alo was confident that it would show up. We went ahead with things as planned. We had Delorah, Buddha, Matin, Hayoolah and myself from the painting. There did not seem to be a need to find you at that time. Alo had given us the bear spirit to help make it to Jewl safe. If we found the unicorn that we needed, we could complete your prophecy.

I looked at your painting carefully. I memorized your fingerprints in case we lost the frame. I guessed where your spirit would be. It required more time than I had. We dedicated our time to prepare for the event. I told everyone, "We shall begin the ceremony this evening. Let us try to get everything ready."

With blink of an eye, the evening ceremony started. Behesht was filled with angelic creatures, including all the invited Angelious. The Angelious, by then, were updated about the mirror Mohabat and her twin sister. The tree spirits shone in happiness and danced. Everyone looked at Delorah with fondness. The trees remembered how they helped raise Mohabat, and prayed for her safe return. We disguised our identities. Both Alo and Buddha appeared in monk suit, guarded by my spirit. As the senior monk, I took charge of the ceremony. I gathered everyone by the Tree of Life and introduced Delorah to the attendees. We all circled the tree hand in hand. I prayed for the angels to guard Delorah against all evil until the end of time.

Then the Angelious greeted Delorah. They all welcomed her to their team. Delorah's tears of joy were soon replaced with laughter. Flying creatures arrived to greet Hayoolah. They asked everyone, except Delorah, to step away from the tree. A strong wind began to move through the crowd. A creature as bright as the sun landed close to Delorah, blinding everyone but me. It was a unicorn—or so we thought.

I spoke up thanking everyone for attending. I informed the guests that the last part of our ceremony would be private, for Delorah and her angels.

Everyone left Behesht elated. They learnt Delorah is the twin sister of their favorite member. They celebrated her righteous return but used their energy to pray for Mohabat's homecoming. Buddha and Alo walked up and joined Hayoolah and Delorah and me.

The bright light temporarily blinded everyone. We witnessed something powerful like never before at Behesht. A white horse with feathers like an angel landed right beside Delorah. The only question on our minds was, "Why does the horse not have a spiral horn projecting out of its forehead?" Despite our concern, we felt confident. It was close enough that we could go ahead with our plan. All the missing pieces as identified in your painting seemed in place. We headed off to Jewl confident your prophecy would come true.

Alo wished us luck on our journey to bring back Mohabat, and returned to his forest. Buddha, Hayoolah, Delorah, and I, along with the white horse, hid in the bear's pouch. We headed to the witch's tree. Matin heard us coming. She peeked out the window to see for herself. Her face lit up. She hastened and joined us in the pouch. The three immortals from your art were now together.

When we reached Jewl, we had to think of a way to distract the two Devols that were on guard outside. While we pondered on what to do, Alo presented himself, accompanied by several aboriginal tribesmen camouflaged in black paint. He sent them ahead to distract the Devols. With Delorah's whispering directions, the bear crept to the mirror room. After checking we were alone, we climbed out of the pouch. The bear spirit evaporated. The first thing we saw was our reflection in the mirror.

We stood in the same place as in the painting. Matin, Buddha and Delorah in a row with me to their left with Hayoolah hovering above my head. The white horse stood to our right near Mohabat in the mirror. We all stood getting our bearings. The horse slowly turned its head to the right. It eyed Mohabat in the mirror and was intensely drawn to her soul. To our shocking surprise, out of its forehead, a spiral horn raised. The horn grew and grew until it stopped inches from the mirror holding Mohabat. It became a bridge for an immortal being to enter.

Buddha moved to enter the mirror. Delorah blocked his way, insisting it was her destiny to save her sister. While they argued, Matin jumped on the horse. She uttered with guilt, "I have an unworthy soul. I am now going to make it worthy. I will save Mohabat," and before anyone could react, she jumped into the mirror from the unicorn's horn. The horse backed away from the mirror and turned toward us—with Mohabat on its back. I dropped to my knees with joy, and thankful, that Mohabat was at last free.

My joy became overshadowed by the realization that Matin was now gone. I tore my gaze away from Mohabat toward the mirror. I saw Matin with her sisters. All three seemed happy reunited. Mohabat, too, gazed at the mirror, resigned to the fact that sadly, she could not save the sister souls. She turned to Delorah who stood beside me. Mohabat smirked when she recognized the glow of a pure spirit emanating from Delorah.

Soon after, tears of joy coursed down Mohabat's face. Her twin sister was no longer a Devol. A female dragon monkey flew up into the air from behind Mohabat. Hayoolah startled at the sight. She described how she met Neyolah during her dreams in Jewl's mirror.

Hayoolah and Neyolah were now free. They cautiously approached each other until they were close enough for Neyolah to recognize the four dragon monkeys on Hayoolah's necklace. She backed off. She recognized the four creatures as her children. Hayoolah remembered Neyolah as his long-forgotten partner. He looked at her with deep shiny eyes. "Neyolah. It is me, Hayoolah, your husband. You do not remember me?"

Recognition dawned on Neyolah's face. She flew to Hayoolah for their reunion. "I cannot believe my own eyes …"

Hayoolah had no choice but to tell Neyolah, "I know, I cannot believe I forgot you. Um, now, how do I deliver this news, it is not good."

"What, tell me … go on, won't you already?"

"How do I say this without … I saw our children turned into Devols. Mahboo and I saw them outside of Jewl. Do not panic. They are not destroyed. It could be that they are untouchable. We are lucky, they are still here. We will find a way to save them."

Neyolah froze upon hearing the news. Mohabat signaled to the unicorn. They exited the room. They found the four baby monkeys playing in a backyard near Jewl. Mohabat used the unicorn's horn to turn them back into little Angelious dragons. She rode back to Jewl in a rush and reunited the babies with Neyolah and Hayoolah.

Tears welled up in my eyes at the scene. I attempted to talk to Mohabat. She looked away. She turned to Delorah, leaning on me from joy. It seemed innocent. I did not think much of it at that moment. We were all happy to witness Mohabat out of the impossible mirrors.

Mohabat left the room momentarily. She then flew back in pulling everyone onto her horse. She dropped us off outside of Jewl and beside the kangaroo bear. The Inuit spirit bear waited for us. Mohabat left. She returned to Jewl with her unicorn. She freed all the tortured beings. I noticed they did not belong to Mohaba. I took all the survivors to Behesht.

The unique creatures did not belong to the regular forest of Mohaba. With a blink of an eye, Mohabat eliminated the two Devols inside Jewl. The rest of the Devols approached to fight. The unicorn used its shiny light to eliminate all the dark clouds and with that, all the Devols.

Mohabat did not stop there. She spread her entire remaining light over Mohaba. The light was extremely strong, causing an earthquake, which, fortunately, did not destroy anything except the Devol species. In a short time, Mohabat transformed our town back to its original heavenly place. The sun appeared. It evaporated the clouds.

We were used to Mohaba being in the dark. We had to shield our eyes from the first sunlight in a long time. The loud earthquake and the sunshine brought all the people out of their homes. As soon as they opened their doors, the town became filled with laughter and joy. The hyenas had been wiped out with the Devols. The townspeople could walk freely throughout their town.

The centuries of torture banished with the people in town not knowing how they had been freed from their shackles. Mohabat reinstated Mohaba's system of justice. I returned with Delorah from Behesht. We heard the earthquake. We worried that the Devols caused another disaster. As soon as I saw the sun, I could smell it in the air that Mohabat saved us.

I transformed into a black flying spirit horse that Alo created for me and caught up to Mohabat. I tried to pull her from her horse. Mohabat coldly looked at me. She looked down on the ground where Delorah stood. She turned her face back to me. "Try to think of me fondly as we say our goodbyes, Mahboo. Remember me occasionally when you ever find that silent moment. Take care of yourself. Also, remember to not forget to watch out for all those evils out there thooooohhh, goood byeeee."

I begged, "Please do not leave me. Mohaaabaahtttt. Please, you need to hear me before you go. Come onto my horse, now. You can fly away after. Let me talk to you. Please, do not do this to me. I cannot lose you. Moohhhhaaabaattttt. Damn it."

Mohabat flew away, ignoring my pleas.

Delorah shared with me later that Mohabat approached her near the forest. She asked her for a favor and that gave me up to her. Mohabat said to her, "Take good care of Mahboo for me, dear sister. He is yours now." I could guess what she had been thinking. I do not think and hope she was resenting her sister. She did look angry. I spent all my time saving Delorah instead of saving her. Delorah now had an eternal heartbeat and a clean soul. I swore to Mohabat to help her with her heart. Not Delorah. Delorah was no more to me than my backup plan to get Mohabat out of the mirror.

Farm, I tried everything. She flew away to parts unknown.

I returned to the forest with Delorah and Buddha in shock. The Devols were eliminated in one fell swoop. If we had known it would be this straightforward, I would have asked Mohabat to meet me in Behesht instead. We would have helped her gain an eternal heartbeat. We would have had the unicorn sooner. All this time we spent training monks for battle. All we needed was a unicorn that you painted. I am confident everything else would have had fallen into place after it. Many regrets ran in my mind and Buddha's as to how we miserably failed to save Mohabat.

If only we had discovered your prophecy earlier, we would have saved Mohaba long ago. At least, we have finally rescued Mohaba. I am grateful to you for your prophecy. You helped save our town.

When the prisoners of the Devols, saw the sun shining, they guessed that the Devols must have been defeated. They returned home to their families. They all waited outside their homes with open arms ready to welcome them back. Badoo rushed home, preparing a speech to tell everyone what had happened. He was welcomed back by his family as if he had done nothing wrong. They had never doubted their son. It was Badoo who assumed they did. Devols planted the shame that had clouded his mind.

With the Devols gone, all the Mohaba celebrated. I felt happy for our town yet consumed by my own misery. I lost the sunshine of my garden. The sun shone while I suffered. I needed Mohabat beside me to witness the victory. "Master, she is going to return, is she not?"

Buddha answered me with a sorrowful tone of voice, "I cannot say with confidence, Mahboo. Before she flew away, she asked Delorah to take care of you."

"I know, Delorah told me."

"Well, it is hard to predict. It is possible, Mahboo, that she might be gone forever."

I could not handle to hear him telling me, "No." With him standing still without a word, I said to him, upset, "That cannot be true. She must be mad at me. She loves me. I know she does. She would not leave me easily like that. She did not hear me. I tried … it does not make sense unless … she must have been mad at me for something. That is it. It is not the horse that took her away. She chose to leave me but … over what. Why?"

Delorah, overhearing our conversation, walked towards Buddha and me. "I am terribly sorry, Mahboo." She gently put her right hand on mine as a gesture to comfort me. "I am not confident why she left us. This was our time to celebrate; look forward to a peaceful future. This is what she wished. I was thrilled to be with my newly found sister. What are we going to do without her now?"

I fumed with anger, "I will not accept hearing anyone say she is gone. You understand me?"

Delorah and Buddha looked at each other and then back at me. Buddha says, "Everyone seems happy except us. We are grieving a great loss, Mahboo. We are."

I agitated, "Mohabat could not have gone far. There is no way she could have last long on that horse. I will find her. She is out there somewhere. I can feel it." I paused for a moment. Buddha and Delorah went silent. "You know what? She is mad at me. I could see it in her eyes. She ignored me. She would not ignore me if she was not mad at me."

"You cannot do this to yourself, Mahboo. I am guilty too. Believe it or not, I do feel this way. If I had not pushed her into the mirror, we would be under the thumb of the Devols. She would be here with us."

"I am not blaming you anymore. We discussed this before. You did what you thought was the right thing to do at the time." Delorah looked at me and said with forced optimism, "We will bring her back. I promise you that, we will."

I did not know whom to believe. Mohabat was either gone forever or she hid away somewhere mad at me. I came up with a plan to search for your spirit, Fatem. That was when Hayoolah informed me that Neyolah had something to tell me.

Neyolah had spent some time with Mohabat inside the mirrors. She appeared confident that until she got pulled into the wind of the violin, Mohabat had not seen anything from the night she died. She had only seen herself having a conversation with me while she prepared for her wedding. Hayoolah came up with an idea. He believed he could return to the mirrors and join the Heshmats to find out what happened through their dreams.

The three sisters are stuck in Jewl's mirrors. My Asura can pass into the mirror and whisper into their dreams. When he mentioned Mohabat, the sisters started to dream about her. Through the dreams, Hayoolah witnessed the incident of Mohabat getting pushed into the mirror. It appeared to her in the dream that I pushed her and not Delorah. Hayoolah had heard from me that Delorah pushed her out of fear. I discovered why Mohabat was mad. She blamed me for pushing her into the mirror. I knew then what I needed to do. I had to find you. I decided not to share with Buddha nor Delorah what I discovered. I joined them for one last time before planning a big search for Mohabat.

"Are you certain you do not have feelings for Delorah?"

How can I when I have strong feelings for Mohabat? I cannot explain how I feel for Delorah. I can tell you it is not love. I told you Mohabat is the only one in my garden that I want to have and share with my friends. She is that one apple on the tree that I would always choose to pick from all the rest. I can never take my eyes off it. Now, it has disappeared. I need to find it because it is precious. No other apple will ever replace it. Love to me is about not being able to live without. I cannot forget her. If she is gone, I am better off going back to my silent days. I will not spend time with Delorah.

"Even though she is Mohabat's blood?"

Yes, even so.

"I will help you. You have told me your story as it has happened, am I, right?"

Yes. Almost everything.

"Well, this is plenty. I can picture you all. I will create you some paintings. I cannot promise it will turn out a prophecy again."

I have a good feeling that now you know our detailed story, you can draw our future. You have done a marvelous job before.

"I might. You must be prepared that the answer might not be what you want. Buddha might be right. She might be gone. Are you going to be all right with the truth? Accepting it? Whatever it may be?"

Yes, I think I know what I want. Of that I am certain. Do I need to find out if she is coming back? Ever. Fatem, please. I raised your soul. You can help me find her? If she is gone forever, then I need to know so I can plan accordingly.

"I will try my best to help you if I can. But, beware, I painted that prophecy a long time ago. I do not know where the visions came from. You know it might have been another spirit that took over me? I might not be the right soul to help you?"

I understand Fatem. You know us well now. Maybe that

spirit can work through you? Even if it cannot, you are all I have. I have been involved in the world more because of Mohabat. I do not care about Delorah the way I do for her. You know by now. You must believe me. I helped Delorah to save my baby. Delorah has an identical soul as Mohabat but it does not make her into the same woman I shared a great past with.

Without informing Buddha or Delorah, I searched for your soul. I knew if you could predict the future that saved our town that you can help me find where Mohabat is hiding.

"But you do understand, Mahboo, that she may not be hiding. She might be gone."

I know but we do not know that. That is why I need another prophecy from you. I need to find her and explain. I sucked all the fingerprints out of your painting. I saw your past. You lived not far from Mohaba. I found you live now in this village to the south of Mohaba as a poet. I disguised myself in the body of a dying man. I entered your house. You spoke passionately of a poet you admired. Before I took your life to meet your soul, you said something to me about sorrow and happiness. I admire poets but did not care to listen to their words as much. I became more concerned with meeting you, his ancient spirit. I had no other choice but to take his or, I am sorry, your life to wake your soul. I am deeply sorry for that.

Before I took Mashoul's life, or yours, he told me about sorrow. I guessed he could read my sorrow. These words like sorrow and grief were foreign to me before I met Mohabat.

Therefore, I needed to find you. I never killed before. Now, to overcome my sorrow, I have become a killer.

"I forgive you. I am not certain about Mashoul. You did take his life to talk to me. What a messy world we live in, hay?"

I never thought I would be a killer. I have taken the life of a man who was passionate about life. I have become a man that Mohabat hates. I killed someone before his planned death. I am a murderer.

"I am positive you have done the right thing to maybe save Mohabat. Who knows? Mohabat, as you said, has been created by our universal gods. You need to ensure she will be all right out there by herself. That is if the gods did not take her back to the heavens. I will help you. It is too late to worry about a dead man. We cannot afford the time to think about this dead body."

What do you suggest that we do?

"You have told me everything I need. What I need you to do is, award me my next life but with memory. I need to remember all that you have shared. I will not be able to paint her. I will paint here in this house unless you suggest some other place."

No, it should be fine. I looked at Mashoul's entire life. He devoted himself to the gods. He practiced poetry for himself in solitary. He was an antisocial creature with no contact with the outside world.

"Alright then. Please take the body with you. I may not be

able to handle the smell. I need to concentrate on my drawings. I will do what I can but, again, I make no promises."

I spent half a day with Fatem telling him all about my life in Mohaba until the moment I took Mashoul's life. I felt guilty killing a man. I carried the poet's body to the cemetery. I became eager to find out what Fatem painted. I hid the body six feet under. I hoped Fatem could make another good prophecy. After all, I killed a man for this painting. I returned to Mashoul's home where I saw many paintings hanging on the walls. These were the only clues that I had to find Mohabat.

One of Fatem's arts had a woman with red hair. Mohabat's hair was brown. It is possible that she changed her hair to avoid being detected. Another of his work depicted an unfamiliar town with modern buildings. Yet another picture consisted of a light brown-haired woman who appeared to be Mohabat in Egypt. Fatem attempted only drawings of Mohabat. The face was hard to see in some of the pictures. In another painting, Mohabat's back faced to the viewer. She seemed to be gazing into a long epileptically shaped mirror.

I decided to let Fatem live even though he knew everything about my past and all my secrets. Eventually, I left Fatem. I suggested that he finds a new home. Fatem promised to continue drawing. He told me, "All your secrets are safe with me. I am here to help you whenever and anytime. You are with the invisible gods and always guarded. Do not worry. After hearing your stories, I believe in your power and strength. I hope you find your woman. I hope your garden is filled with joy. And, your desired apple on the tree that you keep mentioning to me, as you call her, will eternally remain on your garden's tree."

I did not have time to figure out what to do with Fatem. I knew he had been truthful. I trusted he would not give away all my shared secrets. I knew he would be safe where he was for the moment. I may have needed him again. Keeping him around with his memories would be the best thing to do for all the trouble.

I thought about the paintings that had given me hope. I recalled that I had an Asura now to help me. I needed to find the towns in Fatem's painting. For that, I needed to plan. I had to take Hayoolah with me. I returned to join Delorah and Buddha. They were watching the sunset, thinking of how the sun would come up the next day on a town that had completely changed, literally overnight.

But by morning, I decided, I would be gone on my search for Mohabat. I would not say goodbye to Delorah and Buddha but slip away with Hayoolah to find Mohabat. I suspected from the clues in Fatem's painting it would be somewhere far away from Mohaba.

I met with Hayoolah. He and I went to say goodbye to Neyolah before our long journey. I looked at Neyolah, "I am terribly and genuinely sorry. I know you recently reunited with your husband. I need to take him. Are you all right with that?"

"Of course, I am, Mahboo. I love Mohabat. I am worried for her. I was her Asura, remember?"

"That is right, how could I forget?"

"I want you to find her. I witnessed the battle. The monks and the scary monsters. I hope they are gone. I hope Mohabat is safe if she is out there."

"Buddha believes she is gone forever. I do not think so. Fatem showed me his paintings. She is disguised somewhere in hiding."

"If she is disguised in the painting, then how do you know it is her, Mahboo?"

"I told him all about Mohabat so he could draw her. He is not going to paint me someone else when I trust his prophecies. Hayoolah, when you visited the Heshmats, did you learn anything from their dreams?"

"I have some news. It might not make you happy."

"I do not care. Anything to help us save Mohabat will not bother me. What did you see?"

"We were lucky. They dreamt of her right after I whispered Mohabat's name in their ears. It was easier than I thought."

"Oh good. Does she think of me as a killer?"

"Why would you ask me that? You take lives. You do not kill. We know that. We know you."

"You said she saw the night she died, right Neyolah?"

"From what I remember, she saw you helping her get ready for the wedding. That is all. Mahboo, why do you call yourself a killer? Did something happen that you have not shared with us?"

"Um, I told you, Neyolah. Mahboo had to take the poet's

life, Mashoul, to meet with his soul, the prophecy painter. He made that painting that we used to go to Jewl."

"Oh, yes, yes, that is right. You want me to watch out for Fatem while you are gone? That is his name, right?"

"Yes, we need you to watch him. Make sure he does not go to anyone with our story."

"Why did you keep him?"

"Neyolah, we may need him later to look at the future for us. Until we find Mohabat, we must keep him, my dear." Hayoolah moved from Neyolah's side. He came and sat on my shoulder.

"You forgot to mention Hayoolah. The truth is Neyolah, I never want to kill again. I will not kill Fatem unless I have to."

"I think he has sided with us. He will not give away our secrets."

"But, you do not think it is safer to kill him. I mean, by that, that you can have him live in another life and erase his memory. You can contact him if you need to. What is wrong with that?"

"What is wrong with that? There is a lot that is wrong with that. If I do that, then I have to kill a man twice."

"True."

"First, I kill him and give him another life with no memory of his previous one. Second, if I need to get in touch with Fatem, I must kill the other man to get to him. That would mean killing two people. As I said, I am not comfortable with playing the gods."

"Alright, we understand. I have no problem watching Fatem while you find Mohabat."

"If I keep taking lives before their time, then I am no different from the Devols."

"I am so sorry, Mahboo. You are right. I did not view it that way. I think if you are awarding them their next life, then that is not considered killing. That is how I see it, but I understand what you are saying."

"The thing is ... the reason I asked you about the night of Mohabat's death is because if she has not seen the complete night, only parts of it, she might believe I killed her."

"What? You killed Mohabat? No, no, no, no. That cannot be true, can it?"

"Well, you told me how she saw things from her point of view. I am worried that ... um, if she has seen parts of what happened the night she died, she will never forgive me."

"Forgive you? Of course, she will. You did not push her into the mirror. She will see the truth. And you did NOT kill her. That is impossible."

"I did not, it is true. But from her perspective, it appears that I killed her."

"Oh, no. Why? What exactly happened that night? Will you please share with us?"

"I have told no one except Buddha. But, all right. I will tell you both only because if you find her sooner than me, then you must tell her about that night. She needs to know the truth. I never got to tell her."

"Alright, Mahboo. We are listening. We will never think you killed her."

"Actually, I did."

"What? Did you kill Mohabat? No."

"It is not that simple. It was unplanned. It was an accident."

"Mahboo, you need to tell us the full story. There is no way you could have killed her."

"I did NOT kill her intentionally."

"I do not think you killed the poet either. You kept his soul. But, go ahead and tell us what happened that night."

"Well, I actually am not the one who forced Mohabat to marry the king."

"Was it her idea? In the mirrors, it looked as if you were the one who instructed her on what to do."

"Yes, by then I had agreed. But it was Mohabat's idea all along to pretend to marry the king."

"Oh good, I thought you had suggested she marry the king. Now it makes sense. She looked scared when you were combing her hair. You were not forcing her. You were reassuring her that all would be well. What a misunderstanding. You have a lot of explaining to do to Mohabat."

"Yes, I am aware, she thinks I am evil. She thinks I pushed her into the mirror. That is why I must find her first. I do not want her to make any irreversible decisions out of spite for me."

"Mahboo. Go on about the night of the wedding. What happened?"

"I would have never suggested to Mohabat to do such a thing. I wanted us to get married. We made a pact that we would not take her wedding to the king seriously if it happened that they vowed."

"But, marrying the king. Would that not make her his?"

"We had not planned for her to stay with him. We wanted him to believe in her and trust her. And then I needed to catch him alone. We were planning to destroy him on the night of his wedding before he would, you know … he was an evil man, he had to be stopped. Mohabat wanted to help. It was a bad plan."

"Oh, I see. Hmmm, what a risk you took?"

"I know. He was an evil king and a powerful one. I knew that if I got him alone, that was the only way … I knew he was not just a king. He had killed many innocent people. I always had to clean up after him. That is why Mohabat suggested we get rid of him. We wanted to cleanse Mohaba of evil." I took a break, distracted by my own thoughts.

"Mahboo, hey, are you there?"

"Ahhh, OK. Sorry, well, Mohabat suggested that the best way would be for her to get close to him. She needed to get the king alone and unprotected by his guards and distract him. I would then come and have my chance to exhume his soul."

"Oh, that is why she wanted to marry him. So, you got him alone in a room? Is that right?"

"Well yes and no. On the night of her wedding, after I got Mohabat ready, I went to watch the ceremony. They were not going to be alone together until the wedding ceremony and the feast would end."

"I remember you giving her advice on how to prepare. She seemed nervous. It did look like you were forcing her to go through with it. Now, I understand."

"Yes, disguised as her maid. I saw Mohabat go down the aisle with him. I had no idea until I heard a shout. The king had learned our plans. He managed to find a woman who had a similar soul to Mohabat to deceive me. I could not believe it."

"Oh, you think that woman could be Delorah."

"But Delorah was a Devol then."

"True but she was the same age as Mohabat. They were only 17, right? She probably was not that contaminated then, you know."

"That is true. It could have been Delorah. I cannot tell the difference. They are twins, after all."

"Are you going to confront her about it?"

"No, of course not. It does not matter which woman went down the aisle. Delorah is not a Devol anymore. I promised not to judge her for her past."

"You are right. She has gone through a lot to earn your friendship, and Buddha's."

"Sorry Mahboo, go on."

"Anyway, by the time I reached the room, it was too late. The king attempted to touch Mohabat. He was about to sap her of her soul."

"Oh noooh."

"What did you do?"

"I was clueless as to how he developed such strong powers."

"He may have been working with the Devols."

"It is possible. Mohabat had a beige, mushroom color, comfortable looking long dress other than her wedding outfit on. I quickly approached the bed. I tried to suck his soul out. The king managed to evade me."

"Oh, poor Mohabat. What happened to her?"

"It all happened fast. He moved away unbelievably fast. Without realizing it, I sucked Mohabat's soul out and killed her."

"Oh noohhhh, that is the saddest thing I have ever heard. You must have been going through hell."

"I am sorry, Mahboo. What did you do then? What happened to the king?"

"He escaped. No one suspected what happened."

"I took Mohabat with me to Behesht. Her soul is immortal, thank God. I tried to keep her alive. She died before we reached Behesht."

"Oh no, Mahboo. I cannot believe we are hearing this. This is so sad and Mohabat does not know?"

"That is the thing, I do not know what she saw in the mirrors after you were gone, Neyolah."

"What did you do in Behesht?"

"I gave her an Angelious soul. I am positive the universal gods helped me without being present. I decided that it would be best that she did not remember her past whatsoever. She would be better off remembering neither her tragic past nor me. It seemed better that I would not remain in her life. But, most importantly, I erased her memory to protect her from Devols finding her."

"This is tragic. We are both sorry to hear this."

"I know she wanted to do well. I cannot believe something bad happened to her again. She wanted to help. It is because she always wants to help everyone that these tragedies keep happening to us. She is unbelievably kind. Her kind spirit gets us in trouble."

"Mohabat is an ancient word for kindness. Is that why you named her Mohabat?"

"Yes. She wanted to help me out of kindness last time and this time."

"Well, think of it this way, Mahboo. Her kindness, this time, saved Mohaba."

"True. She got to fulfill her destiny. She is our hero."

"That is right. I am afraid we do not know if she did fulfill her destiny. What if she is hiding from me? Then she could be in danger."

"True. By the way, you did not tell us, what happened next?"

"After I turned Mohabat into an Angelious, I knew she would be safe in the woods. But guilt took over me. She missed living a full life because of me. I had no friends for support at the time. With her being immortal, I was not concerned. I left Mohaba for few days. Few days to get my head around it."

"Was that when Devols took over Mohaba?"

"Yes, sadly. I only left Mohaba for three and half days, to be exact. When I returned, Devols had conquered the entire town. I am guessing that the demon king had something to do with it."

"Mahboo, this is terrible. We will find Mohabat. Do not worry. This time, she will find out the truth."

"You are not a killer. We are not going to hear you say that again. Never Mahboo, never."

"Yes, you took a soul of a poet to help save Mohabat. You are not, and I mean not, a killer."

"She is right Mahboo. You need all your strength to find Mohabat. Then you can ask for her forgiveness."

"We will pray that saving Mohabat is worth taking a man's life. She is an angel. She needs someone like you to care for her. She must be emotional over the trauma she experienced. That could be why she left. It may not be over. You must find out. We will help you."

"Hayoolah is right, Mahboo. She might not know about that night. You can show the scene; what happened in Jewl. She will see, you are not the one who pushed her."

"Thank you—both of you—for believing in me."

"We are your Asuras. We will watch your back. Both you and Mohabat saved us from evil. You brought our family back. We will forever be at your feet."

"I am glad you are helping me find Mohabat. I cannot believe Buddha thinks Mohabat is gone forever. I am lucky to have found you, my Asuras."

"We are lucky and blessed too." Neyolah shared with a grateful tone.

Second, later I hear, "We owe you our family," Hayoolah and Neyolah uttered in one voice.

"Even if you feel that you have not made up for it, you will, once you find Mohabat. You can ask for her forgiveness then."

"I agree. Until then, you shall not worry."

"Heroes are not killers. Heroes are our saviors."

"She is right, Mahboo. Do not listen to that voice inside your head. We need more heroes like you. Killing is sometimes necessary. You cannot let your anger get the best of you. What did you get out of worrying all these centuries over Mohabat's tragic death? Nothing."

"See, Mahboo. I am also siding with Hayoolah. You cannot worry about little things like that."

"I do have to worry. I had a big part in it."

"No, you do not seem to understand what we are trying to say to you."

"I know, I know, I hear, I am a hero. But, you know, and I know a hero never kills."

"I think because you raised Mohabat, you have developed some of her emotions. You need to separate the two. You can feel with your friends and loved ones. That is separate from your duty as Death and using the gift to do good things. There will always be death and sadness."

"Very true, how did you little dragon monkeys learn so much about life?"

"We have a family and partner. That is separate. We can remain Asuras. Our duty is to kill and defend. That does not make us evil parents, now does it?"

"I do understand. I do. My situation is different. If I find that by killing a man I save Mohabat, Mohaba's savior, I promise you, I will not regret."

"Now we are talking." Both Hayoolah and Neyolah encouraged Mahboo to stay positive. It seemed that they knew how to talk to Mahboo.

"She is likely hiding in one of the buildings in Fatem's painting. We must find it. Hayoolah, are you ready for the journey?"

"Yes, shall we?"

CPSIA information can be obtained
at www.ICGtesting.com
Printed in the USA
LVOW03s1620120318
569550LV00002B/494/P

9 781947 488106